I groggily stumbled to the still-pounding door. I thought I had won after the servers at Valente International went crazy on my first day. My apartment (all 7,200 square feet of it) had no computer, no telephone, no tablet…not even a television, though V kept agitating on that point, insisting she was addicted to the infernal TV device. My position was a bit more complicated: technology did weird things around me.

PRAISE FOR THE WORKS OF JOSHUA BADER

TWO WIZARD ROULETTE
Modern Knights: Book Two

CITY OWL PRESS
www.cityowlpress.com

Cover design by Tina Moss. All stock photos licensed appropriately. Edited by Yelena Casale.

For information on subsidiary rights, please contact the publisher at info@cityowlpress.com.

Print Edition ISBN: 978-1-944728-17-5

Digital Edition ISBN: 978-1-944728-33-5

Printed in the United States of America

Two Wizard
ROULETTE

MODERN KNIGHTS

BOOK TWO

JOSHUA BADER

CITY OWL
PRESS

To Robert Pirsig,

For helping me understand who I was

without resorting to electroshock,

And to Dr. Neuenschwander,

For forcing me to make his acquaintance.

To all the Phaedrus, David, and Ruby.

- Joshua

PROLOGUE

Sheriff Nicky Alderman raised the bullhorn to her lips
again. "I repeat, come out now, with your hands up. We
have you surrounded." She was speaking the truth, but it
didn't make her feel any better about the potential outcomes.
She had six officers and two cars on the back alley emergency
exit from the bank; another four cars and twelve officers waited
with her out front. Inside Painted Mountain State Bank, one
lone robber, presumed but not confirmed armed, was lurking,
waiting to make his move.

Painted Mountain State Bank had never been robbed before
and her deputies had no experience with hostage situations.
One robber should not have been a challenge, she thought, but
this one seemed to have everything falling into place for him.
On a normal business day, the bank rarely carried more than
$20,000 in cash. For a variety of reasons, including the
upcoming county fair, they had over $100,000 today, according
to the bank president's estimate. That might have been unlucky
coincidence, but add in the field trip from the local K through 8
school that just happened to be touring the bank, and the bandit
held all the cards. The nearest available emergency response
team was three hours away in Phoenix.

Nicky had run for sheriff three years ago on a platform of
reforming the county's speed traps and focusing on fair and
consistent policing. Insane bank robbers were not a topic

mentioned even once in either her campaign or her opponent's. From the jumbled cell phone reports they had received from the hostages inside, the robber was definitely insane. He talked to himself constantly and was dropping in and out of multiple accents. The reports were so erratic, so all over the place, she found it hard to believe that all of the hostages were really describing one and only one bandit. With over twenty children and a dozen adults as human shields, Sheriff Alderman dreaded how this would play out over the next several hours.

She had just resigned herself to not seeing her teenage daughter before bedtime tonight, when the doors of the bank opened. The man who stepped out was not familiar to her: tall, dark, and muscular, in a no-sleeve black t-shirt, highlighting his threateningly large biceps. A military green duffel bag hung over one arm, bulging with the unusually large cash reserves that formerly belonged to the bank. The chrome of a revolver's hammer gleamed from the top of a holster, dangling casually off the man's right hip, like a nightmare reflection of a young Clint Eastwood.

The deputies snapped to attention, simultaneously crouching behind their nearest cover and training their guns on the robber. Nicky dared to dream that this might be over sooner and more easily than expected. She hit the trigger on the megaphone. "Drop the duffel bag and raise your hands over your head. Do it now."

The man smiled, and Nicky instantly hated how attractive a smirk it was. He lacked the benefit of sound amplification, but she heard his response clearly. "I have an alternative suggestion. How about all of you holster your guns, get in your cute little police cars, and drive away? No one gets hurt, not the kids, not you, and especially not me. You go your way and me and the money go ours."

"I don't think so. I've got a dozen guns trained on you and you haven't even drawn your weapon." She paused. "Drop the bag now and we can make it back to the county jail in time for fried chicken night. We'll get you the help you need."

He shook his head and muttered something to himself that sounded like, "They never learn." He took a step down the bank's stairs as if he were going for a casual walk.

When she tried to recall later, Nicky was never sure which of her deputies had fired first. Within a fraction of a second, it became moot, as all of their guns rang out. All was smoke, cordite, and metallic screaming...and the robber kept walking down the steps. Chunks of concrete and dust flew up all around him as the bullets impacted, but not a single rebound or stray piece of shrapnel touched him. Either all of her deputies had forgotten how to aim in the excitement...or something very, very wrong was going on here.

As he strolled through the storm of bullets, he drew, not the gun from the holster, but the index and middle finger of his right hand, pointing them rigid like the imaginary guns of every childhood playground. He aimed at the cruiser on the left of the ringed barricade and jerked his hand back, then playfully pulled the fingers up to his lips to blow off the imaginary smoke. Nicky Alderman could only wonder just how crazy this soon-to-be-dead man was. Her pondering stopped short a heartbeat later, when the police cruiser he had pointed at exploded in flame, the blast louder and shriller than all of the loosed bullets combined.

All was chaos, then, as her deputies scrambled: some away from the explosion, others toward their fallen brothers, some others simply scrambling like headless chickens. Sheriff Nicky Alderman could only watch, the megaphone dropping from her hand as she reached for her own pistol. The man cocked his imaginary finger gun again and pointed at another cruiser, before jerking his hand in recoil. No explosion followed, only loud hissing as all four tires on the car suddenly fell flat.

She took the time to aim, her bead clearly drawn on his heart. "Put your hands up, now. Drop the imaginary weapon."

The bank robber just smiled and kept walking, taking the

time to point his finger cannon at her. "I don't think so, sheriff. Pretty sure today is my lucky day."

She squeezed the trigger, her gun recoiled…and jammed. She stared at her trusted weapon in utter disbelief. When she looked again for the man, dreading the recoil of his fingers, he was gone. Nicky searched frantically all around, but the crazy, hopelessly outnumbered, completely surrounded bandit, was gone–cash and all.

PART ONE

NEW PARADIGM

"Everyone changes. It's the one consistent fact of life. Even if time were as flexible as a piece of string or a ball of mud, there's no going back to where we were. The events may remain the same, but the person experiencing them has changed. I found that out the hard way twice."

- Jadim Cartarssi, Philosopher and Amateur Time-traveler

1

COLIN

L oud pounding on the front door of my apartment was never a good way to wake up. A timid gentle tap or a rhythmic knock might have been okay and could have meant anything: Jehovah's witnesses, local police, a visitor from the Fairy Realm. Pounding, hard and determined, meant it was Timmy. Everyone else had reason to be scared or polite. The police knew I was in the employ of Valente International, and specifically Lucien Valente, CEO of said corporation. Most cops wouldn't talk to me unless they had an ironclad warrant and a smoking gun with my fingerprints on it. The rest of the cops were on Lucien's payroll. A giant troll could pound on my door like that, but in general, I had found they were too polite and well-mannered to do so. Timmy, on the other hand, didn't care that a mysterious wizard and his crazy assassin girlfriend lived behind the door. He just wanted to make sure we heard him.

Speaking of Veruca, I was surprised to see she was already up and gone for the morning when the acoustic assault roused me from my six a.m. slumber. She hadn't mentioned any work projects scheduled for today, but that wasn't highly unusual. The longer we lived together, the more secrets we kept from each other. I loved V: her rebel spirit, wild hair, curiosity, and lethal talents. But I still had a softy and squishy part inside of me known to most people as their conscience. It bugged me to know that our livelihood required two to three assassinations per week to maintain. The fact that her family had demon blood in it from four generations back couldn't have bothered me less. Believe me, I was living in a heckuva glass house to start casting stones on that count.

I groggily stumbled to the still-pounding door. I thought I had won after the servers at Valente International went crazy on my first day. My apartment (all 7,200 square feet of it) had no computer, no telephone, no tablet...not even a television, though V kept agitating on that point, insisting she was addicted to the infernal TV device. My position was a bit more complicated: technology did weird things around me. There was something about combining a wizard and anything that allowed bodiless voices to communicate through means not generally well understood to the layman. To be blunt, sometimes the dead saw it as a free-range opportunity to call up and express their dissatisfaction with the afterlife. Random dead might have been acceptable, but I never, ever wanted to talk to my mother like that again. Death changes a person.

Lucien Valente, however, had refused to accept that he could have an Inner Circle employee who wasn't available to him by modern communication technology. Enter Timmy, the future community manager for the first floor of apartments underneath me, if that community ever actually opened. A lot of people in the area weren't thrilled with the idea of the first floor of the abandoned motel being turned into low-income housing for recently released sex offenders. I wasn't thrilled, but at least their sex offender registration prevented them from owning a computer or having an Internet connection. The first offenders were still two months away from moving in...but Lucien had brought in Timmy, community manager wonder boy and possible future frog (if I ever learned that spell), two weeks ago. I'm pretty sure the entire purpose of moving him in early was so that Lucien could install a phone line into Timmy's apartment…and call him anytime he needed to talk to me. Best I could tell, the new hire thought of his job as a religious calling and saw Lucien as patron saint. Accordingly, he beat on my door with zealous fervor whenever Valente said jump.

My front door was still vibrating when I turned the handle and pulled it open. I shot out my best death glare, the kind that made most supernatural baddies pause for at least a second or two with dread and doubt. Timmy smiled his exuberant, possibly mentally challenged, smile. "Hiya, Colin. How are you doing? Great morning, huh?"

I looked down at my naked wrist for a beat. "Half past who the hell is awake this early. What's up, Timmy?" I knew the answer already: please call Mr. Valente, at your earliest convenience, from the payphone in the parking lot. Timmy would likely add that I was welcome to use the phone in his apartment if I wanted to stop in, maybe have a cup of coffee. That was always the message.

Except it wasn't the message this time. "Mr. Valente said to get dressed; he'll be by to pick you up in ten minutes." Timmy beamed and held out a ceramic mug with a cartoon of two cats tangled together in a ball of yarn. "Coffee to get you going?"

Lucien Valente, CEO of Valente International, the richest man you've never heard of, lord of subsidiary upon subsidiary upon subsidiary, and employer of demon-blooded assassins, was picking me, his personal wizard, up in ten minutes. I grunted something to Timmy, slammed the door in his face, and began hurried preparations. The shit was about to hit the fan.

2

COLIN

I t must have taken Timmy a minute and a half to make a cup of coffee for me and hurry upstairs, because I heard the precise, controlled tapping on my door eight and a half minutes later. I scooped up my leather jacket, made sure my chaos blade was still in the left pocket, and scurried to the door while trying to put the jacket on at the same time. Before sunrise was never a good time for me to try to multitask and I nearly tripped over the newly installed humidity- regulated scroll case. Still, I survived to open the door. I was surprised, but not shocked, to find that Lucien had climbed the stairs himself, rather than sending his driver up.

"Mr. Fisher," Lucien bowed by the slightest tilt of his perfectly coiffed head. "I hope you do not mind the intrusion. I would not have bothered you so early if it were not urgent."

Valente was, as always, immaculately put together. He was the absolute picture of style and grace, with a tall, athletic body in a custom-tailored suit. Today's was a harder granite gray, rather than the more typical silver fabric, but the white Nehru collared shirt with silver jet buttons was his normal attire. I didn't even try to compete: khakis with lots of pockets and hopefully not too many stains from yesterday, paired with a wrinkled green shirt straight from the clean laundry basket. Hopefully my trademark black leather jacket concealed the worst of the wrinkles and any socks that may have been electrostatically attached to my back. Lucien paid me enough that I could have dressed like him if I wanted to, but something from my homeless vagabond days still insisted it was morally wrong to shop at anything more upscale than Walmart or Goodwill.

I nodded back. "Of course, sir. What's up?"

"We can talk in the car on the way to the airport. I need your expertise in Las Vegas."

Lucien closed the distance between my front door and the stairs down from the old motel second floor before he realized I wasn't following him. When he looked back, I said, "I don't do airplanes, sir. Too many electronics."

For a brief moment, I thought I saw a micro-expression of rage on his face before it settled into confusion. Lucien Valente had very little recent experience with people saying no to him. He was the CEO of a multi-national corporation with a unique combination of intelligence, ruthlessness, charisma, and power that made Bill Gates jealous (I knew this for a fact. I had spent most of the company New Year's Eve party reading Mr. Gates' body language). Add in the fact that my girlfriend was not the only assassin he employed, and Mr. Valente was the epitome of the man people didn't say no to. When he finally recovered from the shock, he walked halfway back to me before saying, "We can discuss your aerial status in the car on the way. Let me show you a few things and we can decide on the best way to proceed."

In lower tones, he added, "Given the number of attempts on your life in recent weeks, I would prefer to be discussing this inside my armored limousine."

That gave me pause. The last assassin I had heard of Veruca had killed on Thanksgiving day. Valentine's was right around the corner and nobody had bothered to tell me if anyone else was trying to kill me. Even so, it didn't matter. Saying no to Lucien once was good, clean fun. Twice in one morning and mysterious assailants might be the least of my concerns. I closed the door on my ritual laboratory-slash-home, before thinking better of it. "Be right down, sir."

I popped back inside, grabbed the Tic-Tac-size plastic box off the shelf, pocketed it and headed back out, being careful both to lock the door and to activate the runes on the doorway. Up until last October, I had lived out of a '84 Crown Victoria and protecting my possessions had been a minor concern. Now that I was personal wizard to the head of Valente International, my home contained not just my meager possessions, but a host of weird and exotic artifacts of unknown but potentially magical properties. No one had said to make sure that Lucien's property didn't get stolen, but I had thought it wise to take a few more precautions than when I lived in my car.

3

COLIN

To be honest, I had always imagined that the inside of Valente's personal limousine would be more impressive. It was slightly larger than a normal Lincoln Town Car and in the prerequisite black with chrome highlights, but on the street I wouldn't have looked at it twice. Knowing my boss, that might have been the point. He enjoyed luxury and power, but he also valued his anonymity. State-of-the-art oversize stretch limos undoubtedly attracted paparazzi like a restaurant dumpster summoned flies. As I slid onto the black leather seat next to him, I was pleasantly surprised to discover the leather was toasty-warm despite the early February Boston temperatures outside. It had been a relatively mild winter after that nasty December 3rd storm, when a cannibal winter demon might have become trapped inside my copy of the Necronomicon, but even a mild Massachusetts winter was too cold for me.

Lucien waited till I had settled in before beginning. "Put these on, Mr. Fisher. My hope is that they will delay or disrupt the effect you have on technology."

I was not overly surprised to discover that the black leather gloves he handed me were a perfect fit. They were a little bit over-padded, and crinkled when I put them on, as if there was something else layered between the inner lining and the leather.

"I'll try anything once."

After they were on, Lucien retrieved a large black tablet and began tapping away at the screen. I had loved computers as a kid and would have loved to know more about the strange device, but ever since I made the pact that gave me my magic, technology and I were not friends. After a few moments, Valente spun the tablet to show me a grainy, zoomed-in image of a man standing near a blackjack table. "I need you to find this individual for me, Mr. Fisher."

I studied the face, what little there was to study. He was white with dark, scraggly hair and a goatee. He looked tall and broad, but without a reference to other people it was hard to say just how big he was. "What else do you have on him?"

"That is a large part of my problem. This individual has spent the night in at least three casinos owned and operated by subsidiaries of Valente International in the last week. Do you have any idea how many cameras are inside a casino, Mr. Fisher?"

I took a stab in the dark. "A hundred on the guests, a couple hundred on the employees."

"You're not too terribly far wrong. Given my connections within the Nevada Department of Transportation and the Las Vegas Traffic Commission, I could create a moment by moment picture album of most tourist visits to Sin City. Beyond traditional security cameras, I have infrared and ultraviolet devices, facial recognition software, and a security chief with some unique talents. All that technology, and that's the only picture I have of the individual in question."

I pondered the possibilities, both magical and otherwise. It sounded strange, to be sure, but strange alone didn't mean it was necessarily sorcerous. "What happened to the rest of the images? You should have hundreds of shots of him. Any chance he's bribing one of your security staff to edit him out?"

"Inside job was my security chief's first explanation for it and I have given him ample opportunity to investigate in that direction. Having reviewed the evidence myself, I think something else is to blame." Lucien tapped on the screen a few times and a video clip of Clint Eastwood's famous "Do you feel lucky" scene began to play on the tablet. As soon as the clip finished, it looped back to the beginning and played again. "For the twenty-two hours he was inside the first casino, this is what was recorded by every single camera in the building. According to the personnel who were working, the monitors were working normally...but the hard drives recorded Dirty Harry."

"Odd, but I assume someone with sufficient computer skills could have accomplished that."

"Technology is not my field, either, Mr. Fisher, but there are always multiple possibilities. This is what was recorded at the second casino. Nineteen hours, no overlapping personnel between the two casinos."

The feed had been edited to combine multiple camera angles. A large man in a black trench coat, of roughly similar size physically to the man in the initial image, entered through ornate sliding glass doors and began wandering throughout the casino. The video captured his boots, coat, and clothing, but throughout all the tape a giant yellow smiley face with a bleeding gunshot wound dead center had been superimposed over the man's head. "Again, the workers insisted the live feed to their monitors was normal, but this is what was recorded."

"And his third stay?"

"For the vast majority of his twenty-hour stay, the system recorded nothing at all, only static. Mixed among the nothingness were a handful of images. Only one of those included any footage of our mystery guest and you have seen it already."

I chewed it over mentally. "If it is magic, it might be getting weaker. Some kind of a ritual confusion aura. The further he gets in time from the ritual, the less helpful it is to him. First time, closest to the ritual, you get nothing. Second, you at least get a rough physical description as far as height and weight.

Third, you get a picture of him, even if that's all you get."

Lucien nodded. "Potentially. Are you aware of any such rituals?"

"Of that scope and power? No. But it seems vaguely possible at least."

"I will take your word for it." Lucien paused. "If he is using some sort of magical means to conceal himself against electronic surveillance, could you find him? My security chief and I would both like to have a conversation with him."

I thought about the six-digit paycheck that got deposited directly into my bank account every Friday morning. "I'm sure I could arrange that...But mind if I drive out there? I'm still a little bit suspicious about the idea of flying. You've got enough of a description to keep him out of any other properties you own."

Lucien chuckled. "You would think...but he seems to have strange effects on casino staff as well. When the dealers and game operators are interviewed about him, their answers are all over the map: fifty-year old Hispanic, twenty-year old Caucasian female...one of the dealers insisted that former president Jimmy Carter was the guest in question. I had put out a citywide alert after the second casino. They still let him break the bank two nights later in another casino."

"That sounds vaguely familiar."

I tried to ignore the dark voice in the back of my head. He was sometimes useful, often sarcastic, and always a pain in my ass. I needed to focus on my boss before dealing with my tainted subconscious.

"Sure, sure. Take your time. Why pay attention to the ancient deity in the room?"

I replied out loud to Lucien. "So he could hit another one at any time, if your staff can't recognize him on sight?"

"I'm hoping that, whatever he's doing to conceal himself, your unique talents will be able to see through it."

"I'll find him. One way or another. But flying still isn't a great idea."

Lucien tapped the screen a few more times and turned the tablet towards me. "Not a single disturbance so far, Mr. Fisher. You can use my private jet. I've briefed the pilots to expect the unexpected with you aboard and I trust their skills, even if their instruments malfunction."

The video that played this time was a segment from Clockwork Orange involving the William Tell overture. "When was that one recorded?"

"Two days before his first casino stay, this was captured by an outdoor traffic camera in Kingman, Arizona. What isn't being recorded, but should have been, is a dozen police officers opening fire on a lone bank robber. According to the sheriff, he took out two of her squad cars by pointing his fingers at them, then disappeared into thin air."

"Maybe there's more to life than just a fat paycheck."

"Suddenly turning into a chicken, Yog?"

"I prefer the term 'pragmatic survivalist.'"

4

COLIN

I shifted nervously in the plush seat. It was as far removed from the jet's cockpit as I could get without staying off the plane entirely. Cars had never given me any difficulty, save for an incident involving a mischievous lake spirit. But cars, even really nice cars like my '64 Mustang Dora, rarely went faster than a hundred miles an hour and, if the engine died, the worst that might happen was a rear-end collision. If the plane's engines died mid-flight...my mind filled with stock footage of a cartoon coyote plummeting off the edge of a giant cliff, complete with puff of dust on impact.

"Really? You think I would let us both plummet to our doom? If you die, I'm back to being stuck on the other side of the walls of the universe."

I think everybody has a dark, cobwebby voice buried deep in their minds. Most of the time it's just their own subconscious. In my case, it's Yog Soggoth, an ancient Lovecraftian horror invading our reality through me, after I accidentally made a pact with him one fateful night when I was a sophomore at Harvard.

"You know, you didn't have to drop out. We would've made a hell of a psychiatrist. Could have had a great time showing phobia patients something to really be afraid of."

"You ate my fiancée. Made me think I was going insane and nearly convinced me I had killed her myself."

"Technically, if we're one combined entity in the eyes of the law, you did."

"Shut up."

"I mean, really, where else would I get hands to sprinkle on the Worcestershire sauce before I ate her?"

"Shut. Up. Now."

Yog Soggoth sulked off to whatever hidden crevice between my amygdala and hypothalamus he dwelled in when he wasn't busting my balls. My lingering anger at him distracted me from my absolute terror of flying until we were already cruising at thirty thousand feet. Maybe that was his plan from the beginning, to keep me on the plane and to stop me from thinking about the possibility of free-fall speed inside a metal tube. Maybe he simply saw an opportunity to torture me. I'd shared a body with him for nearly four years and I was only just beginning to understand his logic.

I distracted myself from both the motives of an elder aberrant god and the physics of flight with the contents of the plastic case I had grabbed from my arcane trinkets collection. Lucien Valente had a hunger for the supernatural and collected employees with demon blood, fae blood, and psychic talents. He had also amassed entire warehouses of items that were, or could be, haunted, possessed, or cursed with a mysterious provenance. This particular pair of six-sided dice fell into the odd origin category. Supposedly, Frank Sinatra had been carrying them in his pocket when he first recorded "Luck Be a Lady". From there, they had made their way into the pockets of a low-level mobster known as Frankie the Fish, who made quite a legacy in underground craps games for himself with the dice. They weren't loaded, at least not in the traditional sense: they weighed out and were correctly balanced. But they had made some legendary runs in both directions: some days if you rolled with them, you couldn't lose; other days, you couldn't win.

Their luck ran as far hot or as frozen cold as it got, but never in between.

Luck magic was something of a specialty of mine. I had gotten some pretty spectacular results, such as acquiring my '64 ½ Mustang on the positive end and a client that had won big on the roulette wheel before luck straightened itself out in the form of a speeding bus on the other end. I had studied the dice's aura a little, rolled them around just for fun, but I still couldn't make up my mind if they really were magic or not. Still, since I was heading out to Las Vegas, I might find a few good uses for them.

I was a little nervous about the flight and about any job Lucien Valente handed me. He had a tendency to not send me in unless all other options had been exhausted, which generally equaled out to me being expected to wizard my way through the impossible. But really, I was starting to get excited. I had never darkened the doors of Sin City before. The trip could be just the relaxation I needed.

5

JACOB

The man in the black leather trench coat paced nervously around the baggage claim of McCarran International Airport. Nerves were a strange thing. He had faced down a firing squad of trigger-happy deputies, as cool as a cucumber. But waiting on her plane from Oklahoma City had him on edge. Would she be happy to see him or would they pick up their argument right where they left off two weeks ago? Did she actually get on the plane or did she chicken out at the last minute? Everything had been going so well since his ascension, but would his phenomenal luck still work on his behalf a thousand miles away? Her plane, assuming she was on it, had landed two minutes ago according to the screens around the terminal. There was nothing to do but wait to see if she made her way to the baggage claim.

Maybe it was a sign from the Goddess that the airport was located in unincorporated Paradise, Clark County. Jacob liked reading into the little things to try to predict what the universe was up to. Sometimes it worked; other times he just saw what he wanted to. He fidgeted as he paced, one hand absentmindedly caressing his chaos blade in the left hip pocket. He was not much of a believer in the rules, but he had at least enough common sense not to take his revolver into an airport.

He was so close to completing his goal, about three-fifths of the way to fifty million.

Five minutes of forever later, he saw her. Looking at Lilianna was like entering the gates of heaven. His heart raced, his face flushed, and a flight of a thousand butterflies ascended from his heart. So strong, so potent was Jacob's magic, a handful of actual butterflies, dressed in Solomon's beauty of colorful array, fluttered their way free from the folds of his coat in an unintentional magical release. He was pleased to see that her face, with those brilliant hazel eyes, lit up for him as well. For a brief moment, nothing else existed for either of them in the entire airport. He reveled in how close he was to having enough money for the two of them to never have to worry about anything ever again.

Reality came back to Jacob, if ascended avatar wizards had such a thing as reality, as he rushed towards his Lily…and noticed who else trotted along dutifully behind her. He had sent one ticket to her, but Rebecca had found some way to tag along with her anyhow. His excess overflow of magic, having materialized so soon in beauty, was mercifully not dripping with enough juice to randomly blast her. He fell into Lily's hug, but his eyes shot daggers at his former friend and roommate.

Lilianna's voice pulled back his focus. "So good to see you, Jacob. I've missed you so much."

He smiled. "How did you know it was me?"

"I can just tell. David stands a little straighter and has his nose stuck up in the air. And Reverend would have skipped on his way over to me."

"Fair enough, Lily." Even her touch couldn't completely distract him from his previous irritation. "Rebecca."

"Jacob." Rebecca's eyes mirrored back his death glare. "So we're out here. What did you want to tell her?"

Never being a fan of conflict, Reverend took over control of the body, shaking off her icy tone with carefree ease and a twitch of what had formerly been Jacob's neck. "All in due time, my child, all in due time. Shall we away to our chariot? I have a suite reserved for us that should prove far more leisurely than some crowded airport."

Lily blushed. "Hi, Rev. Are you guys still all right? Seemed like Jacob was starting to lose it when…."

She let the words trail, but they all knew what she meant.

"Verily, my dear. It will take a lot more than a little eviction notice to wear us down. But come; wonders await."

As they left the baggage claim, Reverend heard Rebecca mutter under her breath. "Yeah, I'm wondering already."

6

COLIN

Valente's personal Gulfstream was over mid-Ohio before I really relaxed enough to enjoy the experience. The chair I sat in was easily counted among the most comfortable I had ever been cradled by. I had no desire to own a jet of my own, though I probably could have gotten one with what Valente paid me, but I did wonder if they sold the chairs separately. I could put it and a mini-fridge by the eastern window of my apartment, next to the magic carpet and prayer rug displays. That combination might have made even me a morning person.

Lucien hadn't been terribly specific, which was nothing new. My boss dealt in secrets, maybe even more than in stocks. I chuckled, remembering my first assignment for him. Compared to the wendigo, I had most of the details I needed for this job. Back then, I thought by a curse, he meant erectile dysfunction or something of that caliber, definitely not a salivating ball of monstrous winter demon. Lucien hadn't been very forthcoming about the whys with that thing with that serial rapist thing in January, either, but I had hunted the pervert down anyway. My boss sometimes described himself as "the -devil you know", but it seemed to me that getting rid of ancient demons and men who preyed on teenage girls was not very hellish at all. Maybe Lucien saw my work as some form of penance for the guns and drugs he ran elsewhere on the globe.

"Or maybe he's making certain of our loyalty before he breaks out the really dirty stuff. I can't wait."

"Hey, he let us take the job with a morality clause included. If I ever find his request ethically objectionable, I can walk away."

"True…but he didn't say anything about not shooting us as we walk away. You really think he would let us quit?"

"Maybe, maybe not."

There was a reason I had been hiding stacks of cash each week in Dora's trunk. The day might come when we needed to run, and fast. I wasn't overly excited about this particular assignment, just because it smacked more of mob enforcer than exorcist. The target was definitely cheating the casinos out of their money…but there were also a lot worse people he could have been stealing from. Lucien hadn't asked me to deliver the kid hog-tied to the nearest knee-breaker; he just wanted it to stop and to know how he was doing it in the first place. I thought I could deliver that without tainting my soul any more than it already was. From the sounds of it, Trench Coat Guy had rolled in to town with a couple hundred grand and had rapidly spun it into…I didn't know how much, but I was pretty sure Lucien wouldn't call me in unless we were talking tens of millions of dollars.

I wanted to start my investigation with his security chief, find out exactly how much they'd lost, see if he had any theories about what was going on. Maybe I'd get lucky and there would be word of another casino suddenly losing bank to a stranger. If not, I could break out the tracking spells, maybe conjure up a low-level fae or two for a spiritual perspective. The fae were not to be trifled with, but I felt I could handle a few simple deals: Sir Kerath, the Unseelie Court's Ohio State Law School-educated ambassador to the mortal world, still owed me a favor from our last go-around. He could more than cover my debt if I slipped up with the fae.

But beyond that, where had this guy come from? Big, magical players with a couple hundred thousand in their bankroll didn't just suddenly materialize out of nowhere.

"Unless he's a planeswalker. Maybe he's just visiting from the universe next door."

"Where did he get the cash from? Think otherworld cash would make it past the eye of a wary casino cashier?"

"Probably not…though this guy seems to have perception distortion on lock. Might want to study up on the Necronomicon's spell for maintaining personal mental acuity."

"I left it behind."

"I know. I just like rubbing in how useful it would be to have it with us."

"The incantation you mentioned basically amounts to stabbing myself in the leg to fend off the effects of insanity and enchantment. I'll pass."

"One of these days, you're going to pass on that book when you shouldn't…As we lie there dying, I'll make sure to taunt you with how I'll choose my pact partners more carefully in the future."

"Yeah, yeah, because people are just lining up to let tentacle aberrations crawl into their brain meat."

I eyeballed the phone built into the table. It looked very much like a landline, which was generally safe for me to use, but surely this high up in the sky it had to use that ominous shadow-worldy Internet thing somehow. Still, accidentally talking to the dead was starting to sound way better than twiddling my thumbs and talking to myself. I got up from the chair, plopped on the loveseat next to the table, and picked up the receiver.

"Who do you think gets the bill for this? You really want Valente to see that you called an FBI prefix?"

I ignored him as best I could. Where there were large amounts of money obtained through questionable means, the FBI might know more than I did. I dialed the only Quantico-area telephone number that I knew by heart.

There was absolutely no response from the phone at first, and I braced myself to talk to a random phantom from the netherworld. A few seconds later the ringing came, soon answered by, "Special Agent Devereaux."

Just hearing her voice made me feel better. "How are you doing, Andrea?"

"On scene, actually, but I've got a few minutes. How have you been, Mister F?"

Mister F, rather than Colin or Mr. Fisher, meant she was surrounded by colleagues who might have known who I was. I wasn't exactly popular among FBI behavioral profilers after their boss and hero got shot just for the crime of standing too close to me. Rick Salazar had survived, but was still on medical leave recovering, last I heard. "Working myself. Thirty thousand feet above the flyover states."

"In or out of a plane?" Outside of the Inner Circle of Valente International, Andrea Devereaux was one of the only people who knew I was a wizard and didn't feel the urge to snicker. She had seen me work enough magic that she genuinely thought it was possible that I was soaring high without a plane. Most of my magic tended towards luck-bending, emotional manipulation, or divination, but I didn't think it would hurt to let her imagine I was a tad more powerful than I really was. Might make her think twice before she decided to try to pin Sarai's murder on me again.

"In. My arms were too tired from last time." Quick beat, then to the heart of the call. "Look, I'm curious if the FBI had any reports of surveillance systems or alarms gone wacky in the Southwest United States. I know it's kind of a broad question, but something totally weird or inexplicable out of California, Utah, Nevada...."

"Arizona. How on Earth do you know about that?"

"You first."

She insisted, "Not the way this works, Col...err, mystery caller. Tell me what you know and why you're interested and I'll decide whether I can tell you anything at all."

"I saw some footage of the William Tell overture out of Kingman, Arizona. I've got some equally weird stuff out of a couple of casinos in Vegas."

"Damn." She sighed, then grunted, and I heard her shuffling about in the background. A minute later, "All right, Colin, let's talk. I've got a little more privacy now…so this guy graduated from a couple of convenience stores in Oklahoma, Texas, and New Mexico to a jewelry store in Phoenix and the bank in Kingman. Eight crime scenes total and do you know how much useful evidence we've got? Zero, zilch, nothing. Not a single working security camera, no physical evidence, no fingerprints, no fibers, and even with the witness descriptions it's hard to be sure that it really is the same guy. The only thing that ties them together is how absolutely crazy the cases are."

"He's been playing in the big leagues with some Valente International casinos this week. I'm heading out there to see what I can come up with. Tall, broad shoulders, and likes wearing a trench coat sometimes is about all I've got to work with."

She sounded relieved to know I didn't have everything wrapped up already. I suspected there was still some jealousy about how I was always a step ahead of them with the wendigoes in Oklahoma last fall. "Might be working with a female partner is all I can add to that. Two of the victims described a redheaded girl with him: young, bubbly, valley girl sort. Possibly with horns and fiery wings according to one of the clerks, though he got hit pretty hard on the head. That help you any?"

"I really don't have a whole lot to go on just yet. It'll still be a couple hours till I'm in Vegas. But it wouldn't shock me to find supernatural involvement somewhere in this mess."

There was a long pause and I worried that my bad phone luck had finally caught up with me. Then she came back with, "You want me to drive up there and meet you? Kingman is just a hundred miles south. Maybe we can work this out together."

"I don't know. Mr. Valente might not like an FBI agent crawling around his casinos."

"I don't like a civilian, wizard or not, looking into FBI cases. Together, maybe we can catch this guy and make sure he gets justice in a courtroom rather than a shallow grave under the sands."

I considered for a moment. I was nervous about it for reasons that really had nothing to do with Lucien Valente, but I couldn't quite put my finger on it. My assassin girlfriend might not like me running around Vegas with someone other than her, but Agent Devereaux and I were just friends, right? "All right. I'll be landing at McCarran International. See you at the airport?"

"I'll have to sell my boss on it, but I think they would agree to just about anything to get a lead on this case. I'll call you back if I can't make it."

It was only after we hung up that I pinpointed what set me on edge about it. Agent Devereaux and I might just be friends…but she was the spitting image of my dead fiancée, Sarai, a fact the FBI had tried to use to manipulate me into confessing to crimes I hadn't committed. I hadn't admitted it out loud, but the resemblance was so uncanny that I felt things for Andrea Devereaux just by association.

"Afraid I'll eat her, too?"

7

DIZZY

Dizzy stood tall and proud in her human form, her pseudo-seventeen-year-old body decked out in the latest Vegas strip fashion. While she'd been shopping with Jakey-poo, no less than four men had mistaken her for a hooker. By human standards, she should have been at least a little offended. But the succubi-blooded chaos demon could only feel proud that she still had what it took to entice and entrap male mortals. Some of her kind thought it was all about getting the body form right, deciphering what was "hot" this century. But she knew better: it was the total package. The trick was to radiate a certain star quality mingled with imitation of innocence to really loop in her victims. Having the right breast shape or ass mold was optional once she got the personality down pat.

She shivered a little, despite the intense flames burning throughout the chamber. She couldn't see her mistress, but the temperature always dropped, just a little, whenever Lilith drew near. The word, when it came, was like a razor blade of ice on her skin. "Report."

"The Hand is in Vegas, as you asked. I suggested he fly in his ex-girlfriend for a little extra recreational fun. Should keep him grounded and in the city long enough for this other knight to catch up to him." Dizzy's orange-red ember eyes darted around the chamber, more out of habit than any real desire to learn about this particular hellhole. "Just between you and me, he's getting a little boring. I wish you'd let him move on. He's more fun when we're free-ranging it."

"Will your goddess let him maintain his power a little longer? I know her affections are fickle, but I need him to stay the Hand a while longer."

"So he can win, right? Yeah, I'm sure Er…." Dizzy caught herself before she said the name. Lilith was really picky about not wanting any other power's name uttered in her chambers. "My Goddess will let him keep it till after the fight. And then you and I are done, right? 'Cause if she knew I was moonlighting on her for you…."

Her skin, even in the midst of Hell, goosebumped from the cold. "The worst she could do to you is only a hollow shadow of what I will do if you fail me, Dizzy. Now go…make sure he stays put long enough for the Lord Knight to find him."

"Yes, my mistress. I'll make sure Darien wins." Dizzy was all too happy to teleport away, back to her Jakey-poo and the land of a million neon lights in a city that never, ever slept.

Lilith sighed as Dizzy faded out. She could just barely make out what the Queen of Hell muttered to herself. "It doesn't matter who wins. Just so long as I'm rid of one of them. Two Atlantean knights is one too many."

PART TWO

VEGAS BY NIGHT

"In every world where there are humans, there is always one place that is forbidden, dirty, off-limits. Naturally, this is the most popular tourist destination on that plane of existence."

- Jadim Cartarssi, Planeswalker and Amateur Travel Agen

1

COLIN

Despite my skepticism, the flight to Las Vegas had gone smoothly. The gloves Valente had given me itched like crazy, but so far it seemed like they did indeed prevent unwanted spiritual interference. I folded them up and pocketed them, being careful not to put them in the same place as my chaos blade and mythical dice. I didn't need either of those bleeding into the gloves and distorting their ability. A few more trial runs with the gloves and I might have been brave enough to get one of those iLeash phone-computer-thingamajigs that everyone else seemed to have.

I had flown commercially before, back when my dad first sent me to live with Uncle James and Aunt Celia in Boston. The private jet experience was nothing like the long waits or jostling crowds involved with deplaning a normal airliner. Within five minutes of landing, I was free and clear. I was hunting for a payphone, a task that had gotten considerably harder in recent years, when I heard Agent Devereaux's voice behind me. "Colin?"

I turned and was glad to see she'd trimmed her hair a bit shorter than the last time I saw her. She'd lost a little weight, too. I was glad for anything that made her look less like Sarai.

"Agent Devereaux."

She closed the distance before a scowl came over her face. "What happened to your ear?"

"Not the prettiest thing ever, huh? Lost the tip of it to frostbite last winter."

"Sorry to hear that." She lowered her voice. "Couldn't you just make it magically regrow?"

I shrugged. "Probably. But battle scars are in right now. I think it makes me look tougher."

"I suppose." Pause. "So where do you want to start?"

"The New Riviera was the last one hit. Security chief is supposed to brief me. Seems like as good a place as any. You know how to get there?"

She nodded. "I may have taken the time while I was waiting to find out which Vegas casinos tie back to your boss. Sahara and the Strip, right?"

"My first time in Vegas, actually, so I'll take your word for it. Let's go."

As we walked, she asked, "I thought you were driving all around the country in that old Town Car of yours before you went to work for Valente?"

"Crown Victoria," I corrected. "Yeah, I did, but I tended to avoid the desert. Her radiator was finicky enough without adding in scorching temperatures to the mix."

"High of 62 today. Joys of February. Really? You've never been before?"

"Scout's honor. Maybe I figured there was enough of a freak show out there already without throwing my hat into the ring."

She laughed at my self-deprecating joke and her laughter highlighted to me that whether I had planned on it or not, I was flirting with her a little.

2

COLIN

The security chief at the New Riviera was not what I had expected. Most of my experience with Valente-employed security experts meant ex-military with sculpted bodies most pro wrestlers were envious of. Ted Darrin was as physically far removed from that description as possible, though I made quick note of the two gorillas who followed him wherever he went. No offense to either of those fine gentlemen, but they had missed their calling in life by not playing defensive line in football. Ted, on the other hand, was nearly a foot shorter than me, barely 115 pounds soaking wet, with thick plastic glasses and a face full of acne. Appearances aside, he was smart and sharp, answering most of my questions from memory.

"So the subject got a room for the night, spent an hour or so at each place unpacking, stalking the buffet line, or listening to the lounge singer, and then he started gambling? How are you so sure of his timeline without your security system?"

Mr. Darrin pushed his glasses up his nose and looked me in the eye. "It took a little bit of leg work. My employees, guys that I trust to remember the details, were getting them all wrong when it came to him. Some remembered the trench coat or how big he was, but race, hair color, eye color, even gender were all over the map. Then I found out about her."

"Her?"

"Girl that was with him. Redhead. Real looker. Pretty good agreement that her name was Diz or Dizzy. Sort of girl who could have made a lot of money working one of the clubs, if you know what I mean. I couldn't get people to remember the guy straight, but all of my male employees remembered her. And she was all over him after he checked in."

"After he checked in? They didn't come in together?"

"Nope. Best I can tell, she showed up at the casinos about a half-hour after he did each time. I thought she might be a professional, but I've been running her description by all the escort agencies and services. Nobody claims her."

Devereaux hopped in. "Do the escort agencies usually give you a straight answer?"

"Maybe not to you cops. But yeah, they usually give me the skinny. I warn them if a guy at our hotels is a little too rough with a girl so they don't send one to him. In exchange, they usually help me out if I'm hunting for a little information."

"How do you know she's a cop?" I asked.

"Practice. I've been doing casino security for over seventeen years now, most of it for Valente. I can spot a cop or an ex-felon a mile away."

Not entirely believing him, I relaxed my vision and looked past him, almost through him, right in the middle of his forehead. His aura was not particularly bright or strong, but it was sharp, almost crystalline, and solidly green in color. I had never seen anything like it and wasn't entirely sure what it meant. I was pretty sure Ted Darrin was not entirely human, but that didn't leave me with any strong feeling for what he was.

I commented to keep the conversation going as I pondered his aura. "Nice skill to have. Agent Devereaux is looking for our guy for similar reasons, mostly dealing with how he got the money he wagered to start with."

Ted nodded, his glasses slipping down a little as he did. "Sure. Guy cheats to get 29 million, he probably didn't play fair to get the hundred grand he started with."

"So walk me through it. Where was he making his money?"

"Started with the roulette wheel every time when he was ready to gamble. Gets down with his warmup, then he'd smack down ten dollars, twenty dollars, forty dollars on single number bets. It's a total shot in the dark, but the payout's 35 to 1 if you hit. Lost every single one of those chump bets. Then he breaks out $1,000 in chips, puts it on 5, his lucky number. It was always number 5 whenever it was time to skin us. Bam. Ball lands in the 5 pocket, and all of a sudden we got a VIP. He stops playing roulette and starts working the room with his $35,000: craps, blackjack, poker. He's tipping like crazy, giving chips away…and still his stack is steadily growing. He's losing, but not enough and not often enough. His wins cover his losses, slowly building the base. We're comping him everything: chocolate, wine, food, and lots and lots of shots of liquor. Normally that works on the lucky ones. Get them drunk enough and they'll give it all back plus the shirt they're wearing. Not this guy. He plays all night, drinks everything we give him like he's part fish, and he's still got a fat stack in the wee hours of the morning. Dawn gets close and he goes to cash out. Every time he pretends like he's really ready to cash out. It's a great routine, I'll admit. Manager stays in his ear, trying to get him to keep playing, give the house a shot at its money back. Guy reluctantly, oh-so-fake hesitation, breaks down, agrees, says he'll let it all ride on one last bet. When he plunks it all down on lucky number 5 back on the roulette table, it's way past the maximum bet limit, but the manager is so happy to be getting the chips back in play, he signs off on the bet: all three times, at all three casinos. The whole night's winnings get multiplied by 35 and the manager is too busy thinking about the job he's about to lose to stop the guy from cashing out or to give me a call."

"Why did they sign off?" Devereaux asked. "I mean, I can see it happening once, manager is too impulsive, maybe he's had a little too much to drink himself. But all three of the managers?"

"Look, repeat this outside of this room and I'll call you a filthy liar. I never said it, capiche?" Ted waited till we both nodded before continuing. "The pit boss has a kill switch. If there's too much juice on the wheel, he hits the switch, 99.8% chance that ball goes in the double zero pocket and house wins. Manager signs off on the bet, signals the pit boss, and assumes it's a sure thing that we're getting the money back. Ball falls in the five pocket anyway."

"So, the game is rigged," Devereaux said, clearly unhappy about it.

"Yeah, but this guy, however he was doing it, had a whole lot more juice than the pit boss's switch." He shakes his head. "29 million in one week. Sad thing is, we're still in the profits for the last year...but we won't be if he hits us again. I've explained the situation to every roulette guy, every pit boss, every floor manager, in the company. But this trench coat guy and his hot looker of a girlfriend are so slick, so charismatic, I'm still worried they'll find a way to hit us again."

"Not if we find him first." I tried to project a sense of confidence. "Take him down for armed robbery, get him out of your hair." I paused. "If you were this guy, what casino would you try next?"

"Something in Monte Carlo. No way he gets away with the same thing here, Valente casino or not. I don't know how he's hiding from us, but we'll find the redhead. Goddammit, we'll find the redhead."

3

REBECCA

"Really, Anna? You're buying the crap he's selling? What about that redheaded bimbo he showed up with at Lake's party?"

Lilianna shrugged. "Look, he said they were just friends, we were broken up at the time anyway...and the money's real enough. They wouldn't let us stay in the presidential suite if he couldn't pay for it. Movie deal for the film rights to Borderline makes sense. How else would a struggling writer go from evicted to millionaire in two weeks?"

Rebecca rolled her eyes. "Guy with multiple personality disorder, dissociative identity, whatever the hell you want to call it, submits an idea and a partial script to an agent, and hits the jackpot? Why on Earth would any studio spend that much money on something that wasn't even finished?"

"Look, I agreed to let you come just in case he was dangerous or lying about the situation. He's not." Lilianna paused. "And now you're jealous. You never worried about my dissociative identity disorder or his when we were all living together, when he kept a roof over our heads and fed us. You got used to having me all to yourself and now you're worried that I'm going back to him."

"Are you?" she demanded.

Lilianna didn't stop to think about it long. "Yeah, yeah I am. That doesn't mean I'm done with you. You're the first girl I ever really…loved, you know. But I love Jacob, too. The only reason we broke up was because we lost the apartment: you think that's ever going to be an issue again?"

"Maybe." Rebecca's tone was lush with bitter hate. "Money comes and goes. If anybody could blow through 25 million dollars, Jacob Darien could. Have you seen the way he's tipping? Bellhop glances at our bags for two seconds and he's giving him 100 bucks."

"Really? You're going to knock him because he's generous? Selfless?"

Rebecca shook her head. "He's the most selfish selfless guy I've ever met. He's got it down to an art." She paused, tried to breathe, ignoring how thick the air in the suite had become. "And yeah, I am a little jealous. He didn't call you up and offer to fly both of us out here to make up. He wanted you; I paid my own way. He doesn't want to get the band back together; he just wants you."

Lilianna didn't mean to smile. The subtle upward twist of her lips broke Rebecca's heart. "It was just me and him to start with. But he'll…."

"You and him and Reverend and David and Ruby and Jade…Goddess, it gets crowded with you two around."

Lilianna rose from the bed to stand beside her, her arms slipping around Rebecca's shoulders. "Just give him a chance, Becca. There are a whole lot of safe, ordinary guys out there in the world. But I promise there's only one Jacob Darien."

4

COLIN

ndrea left me to my own devices while she checked in at the Vegas bureau office, briefing them about a redheaded vixen person of interest. I liked her well enough, but the idea of spending a few hours surrounded by FBI agents brought back too many bad memories. I had spent nearly seventy-two hours in police custody in Boston after Sarai disappeared. I almost had an equally bad run in Oklahoma City last year before Duchess Deluce, Valente's secretary, had rescued me from their clutches and delivered me into Lucien's grasp. Agent Devereaux wanted me to go with her, but I insisted my time would be better spent wandering the Strip looking for our crazy couple.

I thought, when I was still in a limo in Boston, that tracking magic on this guy's power level would be a breeze…the hard part would come after I found him. That was proving to be horribly, woefully incorrect. Las Vegas had a certain air of magic, as if the city itself pulsed with sorcery. When I tried to relax my senses, to let them pull in the scent of magic, the city itself overloaded my circuits. The security manager was a good example. Maybe he was just a normal human, but the years of living and working in Vegas had changed him, charged him. The background radiation of noise, magic, and neon was giving me one heck of a migraine.

I stumbled through the lobbies of Caesars Palace and the Mirage, my senses getting more battered and useless with each passing second. There were plenty of redheads, too, but none so supernaturally memorable as the one I was looking for. Shortly after sunset, I found myself sitting on the sidewalk in front of the Guardian Angel Catholic Church. I'm not sure I would've believed there could be holy ground in the middle of all that noise, but the longer I sat by the church, the more I believed that there was. The grinding in my skull slowly ebbed to a dull roar and my stomach began to settle into a more manageable routine than twister mode. It felt like I was in a small bubble of peace, awash in a sea of storms. I tried to ride the waves inside my safe holy capsule.

I couldn't go into this investigation blind. Looking for a wizard in Vegas was like looking for an ember at a bonfire. Randomly wandering around, trusting to luck, wasn't going to cut it. Luck. I played with the dice in my pocket, slowly clicking them around in my hand. Luck was what this guy was playing with. Consciously accomplishing what he was doing with security systems and people's memories would require juju so big, so potent, it would stand out even in Vegas. But bending luck to protect him, to profit him…it seemed so large, almost impossible.

"But it would work. It's just this side of possible."

"You showing up while I'm at church? That's new."

"Just stay outside on the sidewalk and nobody gets hurt."

"You think he's luck-bending? How? Where's the negative luck going? Luck always has a way of balancing itself out."

"Not always. With mortals, yeah…but not everything out there is mortal."

I chewed on that thought. I didn't like it. Some fairies had strong, positive luck associations, like the Pooka, but as bad as this city was messing with my head, I doubted a fairy could last longer than ten minutes here. But there was something about this case that smacked of the numinous.

"What about a god?"

"You mean an elder god like you? Tentacled aberration, squirming its way back into reality from beyond space and time?"

"Nah, I'm one of a kind. But you humans are always finding things to worship. And worship is power."

Worship was power. Thought forms could store up some serious energy, if enough people believed in them strong enough and long enough. Baal and Moloch might have started as carved statues, but generations of intense belief, belief even to the point of human sacrifice, and their names still had power to this day. I genuinely believed in the Catholic faith…but even if I was wrong, our God had been storing up thought form energy for over two millennia. If he hadn't been real to begin with, He was now, for all intents and purposes.

A god of luck? I tried to think of a few, but found the trivial-pursuit-slash-mythology-circuits of my brain still awash in the dissipating, but still present, fog of migraine. Did Lucien send me out here to fight a god?

"Doubtful. Gods have better things to do than rack up tons of cash. That's pretty much a mortal pursuit. But avatars…."

Whatever he was going to say next got lost to fight or flight mode, when I felt a sharp blade on the back of my neck.

5

COLIN

ombat magic was not my strong suit. Still, I was not a small man, and I'd been training with Veruca. I rolled forward and kicked backward, hoping to strike the legs of whoever was behind me. I missed as they darted back gracefully.

I scrambled to my feet, my hand racing for my chaos blade. Thin fingers laced with iron strength grabbed my wrist before I could get to it. With my free hand, I swung out, landing a solid blow.

"Ow, son of a…." It took me a beat longer to process that I'd just punched Veruca in the jaw. "Remind me to be more careful next time I think you've dropped your guard."

"I am so sorry, V. I didn't realize…." My babbling reflex was in full effect as I apologized.

She shook out her head, her lone crimson bang fluttering free. "No, my fault. I thought I'd get a quick lesson in. Turns out I'm the one who needed it." One hand stashed away her dagger out of sight, while the other felt around on her jaw. "You're turning into a decent fighter, Colin. Wouldn't have guessed it when we started."

"You okay?" I hugged her. "I really didn't know."

"It's okay. I'm okay. I could tell you weren't really paying attention to your surroundings. That's dangerous when you've got assassins lining up at your door."

I kissed her bubblegum lips softly. "But you live inside my door…when you're not on assignment."

"Yeah, well, I'm not enough to stop the rest of them from trying."

"*Lucien had implied something to that end, too.*"

"More assassins I need to know about?"

She ignored my question. "So what's going on out here? I thought you were looking for somebody who's stealing from the casinos, not the churches."

Back to the secrets game, I guess. I missed those early months of our relationship, when we actually told each other what was going on in our heads. "I needed a break. This town gives me a headache."

Veruca nodded sagely. "Neon and hookers. Dangerous combination."

"Something like that." I paused. "So what brings you out here? Other than trying to give me a heart attack, of course."

"Finished my job. Heard through the rumor mill that you were hanging out in Vegas with some two-bit floozy of an FBI agent. Thought I should break things up before you two found an all-night wedding chapel."

I was flabbergasted. "Um, no, I mean, it's not like that…."

"Relax, Colin. Somebody's got to give you grief. I'm just here to help." She kissed me lightly on the cheek, before sweeping my legs out from under me with a well-practiced leg lock into hip toss. She stared down at me from where she landed, on top. "Maybe have a little fun while we're here, too."

6

LILIANNA

everend sat tall in the recliner while he pontificated. That seemed unusual to Lily. Not the pontificating...Reverend always talked, rambled on like a gaggle of teenagers in between classes. He would have hated that comparison, with his highbrow language and Victorian accent, but boy could he talk. It was the sitting tall that Lilianna found strange. Reverend usually slouched, if not downright melted, into whatever piece of furniture he rested on. Then again, she couldn't remember if she'd ever seen Reverend out and about without any drugs in Jacob's system. There were a lot of unusual things going on in Las Vegas.

"And that, dear girl, is why Las Vegas verily is Sin City." He stopped for a half beat to grab the tea pot. "More tea, Lily, or dost thou require something stronger as eve moves swiftly toward night?"

Lily shook her head, wishing her own alters weren't so eerily silent. "No, thank you, Reverend. I'm good." She paused. "Is David around? I haven't seen much of him today."

When she met Jacob, Lily was eighteen years old with a long list of psychiatric disorders: borderline personality, histrionic disorder, attention deficit hyperactivity disorder, bipolar disorder. It was only after they met, and their whirlwind courtship and engagement, that Lilianna had been able to shorten that list to one: dissociative identity disorder. The reason she seemed to have so many issues was because there were so many of her sharing the same skull. Jacob had his DID firmly under control, or so she had thought at the time: There was Jacob, Reverend, and David. His three mirrored her three, so much so that it must have been fate. Two (or six, depending on how you counted) souls from the same pod.

The unusually tall sitting figure opposite her twitched, his head jerking to one side in a rhythm Lily had learned to associate with Jacob's transitions between alters. David, if it was David who emerged, slumped into the chair. He looked smaller, worn out, defeated…traits she never paired with the devious genius who was "in charge" of the Jacob Darien circus. His voice, rich with his usual British accent, had not lost its baritone luster, even if his posture had deteriorated. "Yes, Lily? You rang?"

She sought for the words, but found only Ruby forcibly invading her consciousness.

"Relax, child. Let me handle my counterpart," Ruby whispered in her ear.

David recognized the transition instantly and grinned a shark-tooth smile. "Ruby."

"One word and nothing more? I would've thought after our last discussion you would have had plenty of gloating to do."

"Gloating is unseemly." He gestured around the presidential suite. "I think the room speaks for itself." He hesitated. "And I'm afraid I can't take all the credit for our turnaround."

She nodded, reading between the lines as best she could. "We don't have long, do we?"

"Till Rebecca returns? I wish you wouldn't have brought her. There are enough apologies to be said between us without adding in her."

"That's not what I meant, David, and you know it."

"No," he said, leaning even further back into his recliner.

"Not long at all. I can lock Jacob and Reverend out for a few minutes at best."

Not just Jacob, the host, but Reverend, another of the alters, was challenging her love's mental locks? "I've shut out Jade and Anna." She couldn't help but prod. "I can keep them out indefinitely, if need be."

David, her dark champion, self-proclaimed king of the universe, and arrogant son of a bitch, looked more than tired just then. Ruby realized that this was what fear looked like in his eyes, a sight she had never contemplated, let alone seen before. "It's Reverend, my love. He's strong…powerful."

Ruby was torn between a plethora of questions. She needed to know if the money was real, if it was legitimate, if he was really on the verge of becoming a Hollywood heavyweight. It was his fear, though, that captivated her. "How? How is anyone stronger than you, David?"

He laughed, a short, breathy, arrogant laugh, and swallowed hard on a shot of his drink. "Weren't you all the ones that introduced us to Principia Discordia?"

She puzzled. Religious discussion was rarely David's suit. "I don't get what you mean."

"You should. You should recognize the signs. From fallen reject of the world to luckiest bastard alive in two weeks? Reverend has been chosen."

"David, the Principia is all made up. It's anarchist fairy tales dressed up in sarcastic pomp."

"Normally, I'd agree with you, but argue out of spite and principle." He leaned forward in his chair to whisper in conspiratorial airs. "But in case you haven't noticed the change in scenery…Reverend has become the Hand of Eris."

Ruby, aggressive, manipulative, defender persona of Lilianna and Jade, didn't need to consult with the others to understand what her David was claiming. If true, it meant that Reverend was now the mortal embodiment of chaos on Earth. She shivered and joined David in a moment of silent terror.

7

COLIN

I n a city that saw its fair share of strange sights, I think our table was still noteworthy. I had never eaten at Earl of Sandwich before, but I was a sucker for a good Philly cheese steak. I was messily devouring a reasonably good impression of one.

"For this side of the Mississippi."

Andrea Devereaux sat close on my right, all three of our chairs drawn tight to the same side of the table. She looked every part the haggard, hard-working government agent at the end of a long day, with a longer night still ahead. Not to be outdone, Veruca sat even closer to me on my left. Her wardrobe had undergone a quick change since her initial ambush and her latest outfit was closer to Harley Quinn than J. Edgar Hoover. I tried to distract myself from the tension with mouthfuls of cheese steak and thoughts of my fledgling plan, or lack thereof.

Andrea was relating the FBI's activities. "End result is that the local office is setting up rotating teams to watch the casino parking lots. They're going to focus on the redhead, hoping she'll be easier to find in a crowd, though I wish we had a better description to go by. In particular, they're going to be looking for couples who seem to be in a hurry to leave with large amounts of bags. It's not much, but at least it gets us a few extra sets of eyes looking for them."

"I appreciate it." Chomp, chomp, chomp. "Really, I do." I wiped my mouth with the napkin and elbowed both of them in the process. "But I'm not sure we're going to get them that way. I think we need a trap."

Veruca muttered under her breath in Portuguese, "I can think of a good piece of bait."

My inner darkness was ready with a fast retort, but I occupied our mutually shared mouth with more sandwich before he could add fuel to the fire. Chew, chew, swallow. "The problem is bait. We just don't know enough about their motivations to be sure we've got the right stuff on the hook."

Veruca snickered. "They're after thrills and large sums of cash. Nothing too mysterious about those motives."

Andrea was slower, but more thoughtful. "Maybe. But this whole thing seems awfully driven. They've had more than enough cash to fuel most criminal fantasies for a while now. Why keep going and risk getting caught? If it was drugs, they'd just hole up and shoot up or snort a couple million before getting desperate and trying again."

"I think we split the difference," I said, trying to acknowledge them both. "Money and adventure is part of it, but I think there's something else at play here. Something ritualistic, religious even. We want to catch them, we need a bait steeped in ritual and religion."

Andrea hitched an eyebrow at me. "What are you planning?"

"A card tournament...poker, probably, maybe blackjack. Call it Tournament of the Gods and see if we can't get Caesars Palace to host it." I nodded at my own handiwork as I inspected the pieces of my fragmentary trap. "Make the jackpot ridiculously huge, fly in some pro players. It'll take time to set up, but that works in our favor, too. Feels less like a trap if it's not suddenly scheduled and announced for tomorrow. Shoot for next weekend."

"It's intriguing, but the Bureau doesn't have the resources or the pull to set up something like that."

"No, but Duchess probably does." Veruca leaned forward until her lone bright bang of color brushed against Devereaux's chest. "That's D-U-C-H-E-S-S D-E-L-U-C-E." She returned to her normal sitting position. "You know, just in case the boys on the other end of your microphone need help keeping the players straight."

Andrea kept seated, but I noticed her hands balled up in fists. "What is your issue? I'm not wearing a wire, I'm working with you two…well, at least, with one of you."

"Yeah, that's what all you government types say until you don't need us anymore. Then, it's all 'Oops, sorry, your services will no longer be required, but here's a lovely assassination attempt as a parting gift.'"

I squeezed Veruca's thigh under the table, which turned her wrathful look briefly from Devereaux to me. "Can we keep it down, both of you? I trust her, V. Is that enough for you?"

She sighed. "Maybe. You can be way too trusting sometimes, Colin." She turned toward her FBI counterpart. "Did you tell anyone else where Colin was? Or that he was in town working with you?"

"No and no." Andrea's hands relaxed a little. "I told my boss I had a confidential informant in Vegas I was working with, but I didn't name names."

I filed that particular question away for later and returned to the plan. "V's right. Miss Deluce should be able to setup something resembling what I have in mind. It's got to be a game of chance, it's got to be called Tournament of the Gods, and I really hope it can be at Caesars. I think that combination is our best chance to catch this guy, something he's just not going to be able to pass up, even if he knows that he should."

"All right, I get it," Andrea said. "But what do we do in the meantime? What if he strikes again while we're getting the tournament together?"

"That's a problem, but I don't see any way to prevent it for now. We need more information about who and what we're dealing with. What about backtracking the robbery spree? You said the first one was in Oklahoma?"

The profiler in Agent Devereaux kicked into gear. "Right. The first one tells us the most, because it was the most necessary. We know now he was funding a spree and where that spree was headed. Maybe with that we can dig up something in Oklahoma City about where he started from, who he is, and what makes him tick."

"Get me inside his head and I'll take him down." I nodded and turned to V. "Are you available for the long haul on this one or does Mr. Valente need his art buyer?"

Art buyer was her code word for assassin when saying it out loud wasn't kosher. "Please tell me my assignment is to find the redhead. Oh, and then tell me it's okay if I hurt her a little, while I'm dragging her back to you."

"She does seem like she'd be the easier of the two to track down, even in as big a haystack as Las Vegas. I'm not sure I like the idea of you going after her alone, though. There are a few reports of her sprouting wings or throwing fire around."

Veruca absently stroked her long black ponytail. "Hey, a girl's gotta do what a girl's gotta do."

I finished my Philly and decided to move on to a milkshake. Andrea double-checked what hotel I planned on staying at and said goodbye, promising to stay in touch when she found something. The mood from then on was better as Veruca and I proceeded to playfully taunt each other in at least thirteen different languages. It was fun, it was light, the good old days of Veruca and me all over again.

"Except for the whole secrets thing."

I agreed with him, an act that always scared me. *"Yeah, except for those."*

I waited till we were shambling our way towards our hotel

before I brought up my question from earlier. "Why were you curious about who else Agent Devereaux had told I was in Vegas?"

She grabbed my arm and spun me to face her. "Who did know you were out here?"

I shrugged. "Lucien. Probably Duchess and Lucien's driver. The security chief on this end. Why? What's it matter?"

"Why do you think I changed clothes after the church?" When I couldn't answer, she continued. "I couldn't very well go to dinner with the FBI while wearing a couple of bloodstains. You had an assassin practically on top of you by the time I got there, Colin."

"And you think she set me up? She's the most straitlaced law abiding citizen I know."

"Somebody told them. I don't think Lucien Valente is trying to kill you or he would have asked me to do it. Maybe she said something and it got back to the wrong person."

"What makes you think it was an assassin? Could have been a mugger or a vagrant?" I shuddered at the possibility that she mistakenly killed a church security guard.

"Trust me; I know their look by now, Colin. There have been enough of them."

"What's that supposed to mean?"

Veruca yelled at me, her frustration at my ignorance overwhelming any sense of judgment about the fact we were on a public sidewalk. "It means that ever since I met you, you've had a long, steady flow of killers coming after you. Black slacks, black jacket, white shirt, zero personality. I feel like I've killed the same faceless goon fifty times over. You've got to stop trusting every pretty thing who bats her eyelashes at you."

The wardrobe she described reminded of a truckload of killers that had nearly killed both Rick Salazar and me last fall. "Fifty?"

"I don't know, maybe that's an exaggeration, maybe it's not."

"Why didn't you tell me?"

"I did. A couple of times. But…you always look so disappointed when I tell you I've killed somebody. I guess I just didn't want to see that in your eyes anymore. Maybe I should've taken it like a big girl and told you. You've got to watch your back, Colin. One of these days, I'm not going to be there…and I don't want to lose you."

8

JACOB

"Jacob," David demanded, rather loudly. "We need to talk."

The dark knight protector of the system was dressed in all black, collarless dress shirt, slacks, and boots, with an anachronistic long sword hanging on his back, hilt out to his lower left side. His long black hair was bound back in a silver clasp, the only hint of color among his ebon shades.

Jacob emerged from the mental tower that he imagined as his home when he was not in control of their dissociative system. "Really, David? Can't it wait? I'm snuggled up in bed with Lily in real life."

He sneered, something Jacob was used to. David looked down on everyone, except for his precious Ruby counterpart in Lilianna's body. "You mean Reverend is snuggled with Jade and Lilianna and Ruby? Yes, I noticed."

Jacob shrugged. "Just because I'm not in the cockpit doesn't mean I can't enjoy the view. You know, we all can ride together sometimes. We used to a lot."

"Yes, we did." David's brown eyes, with a red slash in the left, drilled into Jacob. "And then the balance shifted."

"Still salty about Reverend getting blessed by his goddess? It's not every mortal that can say an ancient Greek goddess has seen fit to make him her representative on Earth."

"Because we needed more power? More headaches? I will be the first to admit that there is a certain attraction to the power that comes with being the Hand of Eris." David motioned to the dark storm clouds that perpetually boiled just outside the three castle towers that constituted the imaginary living quarters for the personas of Jacob Darien. "But in case you forgot, we have real power. You and I just have the discipline to use it as needed, for important things, issues of merit."

"That power is dark, David. I still…I still don't remember where we got it from. But it hurts people…Even our best-intentioned magic does damage whenever we invoke that…that thing."

David shook his head. "And Eris' magic isn't? You haven't been paying attention. All that money is coming from real places, real people. Nothing is free, Jacob. Not even our beloved."

"Take that back."

A smirk grew across the dark knight's face. "Mmm. There is still anger in you. Here I was thinking I was the only one capable of that emotion."

"It's not the money, David." Jacob tried to think, to explain to himself what he had been pondering for the last month. "She didn't leave us for the money. She left…because we're not allowed to be happy."

That earned a quizzical look from David. "What do you mean, not allowed?"

"Ever since we made our pact, gained the magic…." Jacob gestured again to the roiling storm in the back of his mind. "Nothing works out for us. Not in the long term. We magic our way out of problems, get things stable again, get happy…and then some new problem comes up, some new excuse to use magic to solve everything. Almost as if someone, or some Thing, wants us using magic and if we stop, it goes out of its way to find a new reason for us to use it."

From the heart of the storm, the darkness whispered, but both Jacob and David heard it crystal clear. *"Look at who is finally starting to think for himself. That could be dangerous, little boy."*

David shook his head. "It's just our subconscious, Jacob. Nothing more. Our psychological damage is so severe that we consciously only function as three distinct identities. Behind the scenes, under the surface, it must be absolute chaos and darkness."

"Sure; nothing to see here; move along."

"Maybe. And maybe it's one giant trap meant to steal our soul or doom the world. Unfortunately for us, they found the right bait. I'd do anything to keep Lily. If that means getting enough money to keep all of us safe and together, without the need for magic, for the rest of our lives, then we'll get enough money."

David nodded and put his hand on Jacob's shoulder. "I did the math. Assuming a normal rate of political uprisings and economic instabilities, $50 million should set you and Lily up for life." He paused. "I feel the same way about Ruby. Nothing good can come from this line of thought, my brother. If she is bait, we are hooked. It may be a rotten hand we've been dealt, but we have to play it now. We have to win her…and we will. We'll get enough money to disappear into South American luxury for the next seventy years. To be honest, I'm more worried about Reverend's instability than I am any trap or inner demons. We are, each, in our own right, very powerful wizards."

Jacob stared off into the roiling mind storm. "Yeah, I know. The power is addictive. I can't deny having a certain thrill. But…something isn't right, David, and you know it. This Tournament of the Gods isn't right. Whatever is out there–" he gestured into the darkness beyond them–"isn't right."

David patted him on the shoulder, before retreating to his tower. "Try to get some sleep, Jacob. That's the easiest way to wear Reverend down. Make him sleep."

All alone in his mind again, Jacob reflected on just how hard it was to find sleep. How long had it been since he'd had a full night's sleep? He stared out into the swirling dark clouds and wondered if something other than him stared back. The last thought he remembered that night before he dozed off was a certainty that he was not alone inside his skull.

PART THREE

BREAKING THE HOUSE

"Have you ever seen a poor casino? You know, one without plush carpets, exquisite chandeliers, and shiny gold crown - molding? There's a reason you haven't. The house always wins. Always. Whenever you're tempted to believe otherwise, take firm hold of your wallet and run the other direction as fast as you can. The house always wins."

- Jadim Cartarssi, Gambler and Amateur Social Justice Advocate

1

COLIN

I t was my third night in Caesars Palace and I was starting to get used to the lifestyle. When I was living out of my car, I spent a few nights in hotels, but nothing quite like the glamour of Caesars. There was a glut of everything there: food, alcohol, music, women. Moderation was still a dirty word on the Vegas Strip. I tried my best to blend in with the other tourists while still keeping my wits about me. That was easier said than done, giving the rolling migraines that continued to plague me.

"Relax, buddy. What would it hurt if I took over for a minute or sixty?"

I shuddered at the thought. My routine was as it had been since Duchess confirmed the Tournament of the Gods was a go: a couple hours in Beijing Noodle No. 9, a walk at random among the many pools and splendors of the resort, followed by a couple hours at the Nobu Lounge. Security knew, vaguely, who I was and, specifically, who I worked for, but I was trying not to be too obviously stalkerish in the eyes of the rest of the visitors. Beijing Noodle No. 9 had a wickedly good sesame sauce and a clear view of most of the roulette tables. Nobu Lounge was blessed with a decent trio of bartenders, a direct line of sight on the casino cashier, and a semi-decent vista over the roulette tables. I knew my sting operation was set for the big poker tournament that weekend…but I'd have egg on my face if the target hit the roulette wheel while I was waiting on the big game.

Caesars Palace is not in any way, shape, or form affiliated with Valente International. On the other hand, what Lucien Valente wanted, Lucien Valente got. It was a longer wait than usual, but three hours after I pitched the idea to Duchess Deluce, she called my hotel room to let me know it was on. Three hours was a lifetime for Duchess, who regularly arranged small miracles for me in under thirty minutes. Small miracles, like having state troopers conveniently evacuate rest stops and shut them down for the night, or organizing company picnics for over a thousand people. The fae-blooded telepath, armed with the name and reputation of our mutual boss, probably had more political power than the president of the United States. Added in to that the mix of brains, power, and charm, and Duchess bore a strong resemblance to Marilyn Monroe.

Our working relationship was fueled by mutual fear and respect. Rumor had it she worked her miracles for me on request, because she feared me more than the rest of the Inner Circle. I had no delusions that she would defy Valente for me…but otherwise she was at my service. When we first met, she had wormed her way into my skull, only to run head-first into Yog Soggoth, who was already in residence. She now stayed out of my head, and really, who could blame her? I wouldn't want to run into an ancient aberration of an old god in someone else's thought life, either.

"I told you I was useful."

"I'm still not talking to you."

"Really? Sounds like you are right now."

"All of this is your fault."

"Which part? The part where you're staying at a five-star luxury resort or the part where you get in excess of a hundred grand deposited into your bank account on a weekly basis?"

"The part where you ate my fiancée and I keep getting tossed in the ring with supernatural heavyweights on a regular basis. That part."

"Minor inconveniences at best. Besides, I also got you a new girlfriend or two."

"Shut up."

Something in my tone of thought must have convinced Yog that I meant business, because he left me to my table game watching after that. It bothered me that no more casinos had been hit since I had arrived in Vegas. Our boy must have been busy with something. Maybe he had skipped town. Maybe he was re-upping his luck ritual. Or maybe he sensed that I was here, that someone was hunting him. Just because the massive current of luck magic that filled the entire city gave me a headache and rendered me virtually blind, magically speaking, didn't mean that my target was stuck with the same handicap. Judging by the other wizards I had met, everyone's relationship to magical energy was different.

I tried to watch the roulette wheel while chewing through some of the possibilities of what Trench Coat Man might have been up to, besides taking millions from the casinos. It bothered me that the Valente casinos could lose 29 million and still be profitable for the year, even if only slightly when compared to normal expectations. That 29 million didn't just appear in Valente company bank ledgers. People, like the tourists and gamblers all around me, had donated it a chunk at a time to the one-armed bandit or the blackjack table. I tried to solve the mystery I had been sent to solve, while gnawing on the ethics of gambling at the same time. Another, very much unwanted, moral dilemma kept shoving its way forward in my thoughts: why didn't it bother me more that I was co-existing with Sarai's killer in my skull?

2

ANDREA

A ndrea Devereaux was sitting in her rental car, staring at the Cherry Blossom Liquortown. It was not a likely target, particularly not for a daytime robbery. There was a Subway sandwich shop two storefronts down, with a good pace of customers in and out. The yoga studio on the other side of the victims also had their fair share of customers. The liquor store proper had seen only one person who Andrea was sure was a customer since it opened two hours ago. An Asian man and woman, both advanced in their years, went in and out on a regular basis, but she was fairly certain they were the owners.

The neighborhood was a far cry from "ghetto" or "distress" or "urban blight," whatever the in term currently was. The people were mostly white, mostly middle-class, mostly law-abiding respectable people. But seventeen days ago, someone had gone against the grain of the neighborhood and robbed the liquor store of one bottle of Irish Cream and ninety-eight dollars in cash. The FBI had later flagged the robbery in association with a spree of other robberies across the southwestern U.S. because of a line in the initial police report about "unexplained total failure of security cameras." As far as their analysts could tell, this was the first robbery, the start of the spree.

The bureau had approved the expense of flying her out to Oklahoma and of a rental car, but her acting supervisor had made it clear she needed results. The action, as far as the FBI was concerned, was in Las Vegas or, possibly, moving westward toward California. Still, they were eager enough to solve this one that they were willing to give their rising star, Agent Devereaux, some leeway. She hated that it took her mentor and friend getting shot and taking medical leave for the bureau to begin to recognize her abilities as a profiler. "Why here?" she wondered, not for the first time. "Why this particular store?"

The answers were not forthcoming from simply watching the store front, so Devereaux got up and walked around in the parking lot. She looked all around, peeked in each store, peered down the block in every direction, trying to understand what drew him here. It couldn't have been the money: ninety-eight dollars was a drop in the bucket compared to his estimated current haul of thirty million. It wasn't a good robbery. It was sloppy and unprofessional and it was only incredible good luck that had kept the perpetrator from getting caught. Maybe that was the point. Whoever did this wasn't a career criminal. Just a lucky kid….

Irish Cream was odd alcohol to steal, too. It wasn't a fix for hardcore alcoholics, and it wasn't the most expensive thing on the shelf. It was the sort of liquor that teenagers might use at a party or when celebrating: sweet and smooth to cover up the alcohol underneath. Did the unsub think a celebration was in order after his crime?

The whole thing felt like a crime of opportunity. The store was there, where he could see it. He needed money, the liquor store had money, though precious little of it, and so he took it. Her psychological training told her that meant this shopping center was in his comfort zone: he lived or worked nearby and traveled past it often. But the sort of man who risked life and liberty for ninety-eight dollars wasn't working; his home had to be nearby. Andrea circled around the strip mall, looking at it from every angle. The liquor store's sign was virtually invisible from the east-west street. He would have been traveling north or south, then. It would have been easiest for a driver heading south on Douglas Boulevard to turn into the parking lot.

It was a long shot, assumptions built upon layers of assumptions, but that was what profiling was, backed by psychological statistics. Andrea Devereaux was in Oklahoma City and had nothing better to chase. She hopped into her rented Ford Taurus and drove north, not sure what she was looking for, but feeling in her gut that she was finally headed the right way on this case.

3

COLIN

Four days down, six to go until the tournament started. I had yet to uncover anything helpful. Veruca spotted what she thought might have been our girl last night, but lost her near the Venus Pool. It hadn't been our best run ever. Usually ninety-six hours would be enough for Veruca and me to take over a small South American country. Whatever form of luck was protecting Mister Trench Coat, it seemed to be keeping us off of his trail, too.

I wasn't sure I could take any more sesame noodles and it was still too early in the evening to be drinking. I had been spending my time that night wandering between the pools and the roulette tables. I knew I was most likely to find them at the roulette wheel, but the pool complex was getting harder and harder to ignore. I've always been a fan of water, whether it's an ocean, a lake, or a magnificently designed interconnected series of pools. Not counting the fountains, Caesars Palace had eight swimming pools that needed to be seen to be believed. The Boston YMCA didn't have anything to compare to even one of those magnificent aquatic treasures.

It didn't really count as patrolling if I didn't get out of my pool chair, though. As I stared out across the water and the dancing lights, it was easy to forget about all the pressures of life. People were trying to kill me. Assuming I believed my girlfriend, lots of people had been trying to end my life for quite a while now. I wondered why so few had gotten close enough for me to notice. Granted, there had been an unfortunate run last winter with a few close shaves: robotic van bomb, truckload of gun-toting hit men. But the vast majority were getting picked off by Veruca before I ever even noticed that my life was in jeopardy. It made me wonder why. Was there some reason they didn't just attack at the first available moment?

"Maybe they know about me."

"Yeah, I thought of that possibility. After the first few tries, they realized that something nebulous, something inexplicable, guarded me against their attacks. It was hard to shoot a guy with an elder god living in his head as his early warning system. Following that train of thought, it meant they kept sending assassins to hang out and be ready for a moment when you can't defend me. Is there such a thing?"

"We're a one-of-a-kind pairing. Never been an elder / human hybrid before. But…."

"But what?"

"There have been other pacts before. Occasionally, a celestial and a human bond. More commonly, demons and humans find common ground. If I wanted to kill one of them, and wanted to make sure I got both halves, not just the host, I would wait and attack in transition. There's a moment when the spirit is taking over the body, but before the spirit can bring its full power to bear, where massive damage to the host's head would kill both human and demon."

I really didn't want to think about the ramifications of that. If that's what the assassins were waiting on, it meant they knew about my darker half. It also might mean that these faceless assassins were really the good guys. If I knew about an abomination from beyond space and time trying to worm its way into our world, I would have felt pretty compelled to stop it. But which one of us drew their ire in the first place? Were they a left-over inquisition that hunted all wizards and my cohabitation with Yog Soggoth only made me a harder target? Or was it Yog Soggoth who was their target all along?

"Good questions. If we could get your girlfriend to stop killing them long enough for us to talk to one, I could ask them."

I was distracted from my tortured inner dialogue by a flurry of movement off by the Bacchus Pools. I missed the sounds, but I could tell from the body language of the twenty-something brunette hurrying away from the waterside that the conversation didn't end well for either of its participants. The girl left behind was sitting in her pool chair, raven-maned head collapsed into her hands. I could feel a pull, a tug, as if magic itself wanted me to go to her. In a split second, I made the decision to abandon my pity party and see if I could help with something simpler than rogue wizards or multinational corporation schemes. In reality, I had no idea what I was getting into, but it felt right.

"Or maybe you're drunk."

"Maybe that too."

She had regained her composure by the time I made it over to her. She wore a good mask, pale, but not too pale, porcelain skin framing green eyes. Her lips were tense, the only outward sign of the emotional storm that had just thundered past. Her gaze was so fixed, so determined not to show weakness, her eyes never even shifted to me.

"Really? Anti-wizard assassins? And you're playing to a damsel in distress?"

I ignored him. "You okay?"

Her head snapped up at me. "Huh?" She shook her head, wet black locks fluttering. "Yeah, I suppose."

"Which translates to no, but you don't want to talk about it?" I paused, lilting it slightly toward question. "I'm Colin."

"Yeah, look, I appreciate it, but…." She sighed. "What the hell, it's Vegas. Rebecca." She stretched out her hand dutifully, with no enthusiasm for the ritual.

"It is Vegas. I can't seem to shake my migraine."

"So you're going to become my headache?"

"Verbal abuse already. Most girls wait till they find out I'm Catholic before they assume I'm a masochist."

She smiled, almost against her will. "You're right. I should've waited till after you bought me a couple of drinks to shut you down."

"I am Catholic and it is Vegas. Seems like one heck of a recipe for drinks. What are you having?"

I could see her turning it over in her mind, debating between the girl who had stormed off and the man with free drinks in front of her. "Screwdriver, easy on the orange juice. It's been a hell of a week."

"Tell me about it." I flagged down the nearest waiter and decided it was time to start drinking in earnest. If the bartenders didn't skimp on the alcohol, my headache might get resolved in an hour or so.

4

ANDREA

Andrea flipped a U-turn and circled back around to the entrance of the Summer Lane Apartments. The first mile north of the liquor store had a few scattered homes interspersed among empty lots. Agent Devereaux had almost abandoned the chase at the next stoplight, where two permanently closed convenience stores stood watch over opposing corners. Not two blocks past it, she drove by the apartment complex. It was the closest thing to a population center she'd seen. From the outside, the buildings were nice, but not pristine. Maintaining a private home required a certain level of stability and resources; getting an apartment could be done with a single scraped-together paycheck. If she had to fill in the blanks of her profile with guesses, she would speculate that someone desperate for ninety-eight dollars had lived at Summer Lane not too terribly long ago.

The complex had gated entry, but the gate stood wide open. From the way the plants grew around the edges, Andrea wondered when it had last been closed. A small wooden sign, slightly faded and chipped, directed her to the leasing office. As she pulled into one of the open parking spots, she observed that the office building was considerably better tended than the other larger buildings. She sat behind the wheel, pondering how she would play it. This was an active FBI case and she was the assigned investigator. Despite those facts, she couldn't shake the feeling that this whole thing was about to left-turn into a dark corner that the bureau bosses wouldn't want to touch with a ten-foot pole. That was what had happened last time she had been involved with Oklahoma City or Colin Fisher. Both of them seemed magnets for the bizarre.

She got out and walked into the office with an air of confidence. A young lady in her twenties smiled at her from behind a desk. Agent Devereaux flashed her badge before the woman could speak. "Agent Devereaux, Federal Bureau of Investigation. Is there someone I can talk to about one of your tenants?"

The woman tried to maintain her professional smile while she pointed back to an inner office. "Ms. Johannes is our resident manager. Let me see if she's available."

Before she could close the gap, an older woman in her early forties appeared at the office door. From behind dyed brown hair and horn-rimmed glasses, she looked Andrea over. Apparently satisfied that Devereaux matched up with her mental idea of a federal agent, she gestured for her to come back into her office. The room was immaculately tidy, with a lingering smell of fresh paint and cleaning chemicals. Not even a single stray paper was out of place, though Andrea would have felt better if there had been. She didn't trust people who had time to be neat.

"Please, take a seat, Miss…?"

"Devereaux. Agent Andrea Devereaux. And you are Ms. Johannes?"

"Emily, please. How can I help the FBI?"

This was where things got tricky. Andrea knew in her gut that she was in the right place, but she had little factual knowledge to conduct an interview with. She hoped she could float her way through this with wit and guesswork alone. "I'm looking for a tenant or former tenant. He's white, with dark hair, about shoulder length, and full goatee. Somewhere in his mid-twenties."

"That's not ringing any bells. I'm afraid I don't see our residents much after they move in. Do you have a name or an apartment number?"

Andrea shook her head, but pressed on. "This guy would be seen. He's big, broad. He would have been late on rent or other bills often. Used cash or money orders, never a check or credit card. Talked to himself, sometimes carried on full conversations with himself. May have had an attractive redheaded girl living with him. And he hasn't been back here in over two weeks now."

The mention of two weeks grabbed the manager's attention. She started typing away on her desktop computer, but there was something off in the way she stared at the screen. "Jacob Darien. Apartment 702. I don't know about a redhead, but he lived with two different women, neither of whom was on the lease."

The way she said "two different women" made it sound like she was saying "suspected terrorist". Andrea jotted down the name and number. "What brought him to mind?"

"We post eviction notices on the tenth day of the month. It's our policy to give residents every chance to make good on their rent, which is due on the first. For each day it's late, there is a twenty-dollar late fee. If we have to file for eviction, there is an additional two hundred and fifty dollar charge added to the total necessary to return to good standing. Two weeks ago, we posted a notice on 702. Mr. Darien showed up an hour and a half later with cash, which we don't accept, and only had rent plus late fee, no extra for the cost of the eviction filing."

Devereaux nodded along and was a little surprised when the manager's recitation ended there. After a moment's silence, she prodded. "What happened then?"

The woman, composed and proper from the start, began to pale and shake. The tremors were minimal at first, but steadily grew as she continued. "I told him, not for the first time, that he needed to purchase a money order and that we required an extra two hundred and fifty after the eviction notice was posted. Standard procedure. He was polite…at first. Said he could get a money order, but that was all the money he had. He asked if I couldn't waive the extra fee, just this time. I told him I couldn't, that it was all imposed from above by our owners. He begged, said he just needed more time. I was…I mean, I thought about giving in, helping. But then… please don't make me remember."

Andrea sat staring at the proof of her hunch, wondering what he could have done that would have shaken the manager so deeply. "Did he attack you?"

She shook her head and began digging around in her desk drawer. When she emerged, she slid a lone silver key across her desk, her hand trembling as she did so. "I…I don't remember. I don't want to remember. My assistant came back from lunch and found me…found me curled up in the corner. Every window in the building, every picture had turned black, as if burned in a fire. He…I don't know what happened, but that man is the devil."

She pulled back her hand from the key and seemed to regain some of her composure. "Take it. I still haven't been in the apartment to pack it up. Scared of what I would find, I guess. Maybe you can find some answers there. I…I don't want to talk about it anymore."

5

LILIANNA

Lilianna noticed a fiery mane of perfectly straight red hair swish across the gaming area towards the elevators. She wasn't supposed to notice that. Becca should have come running after her, apologized, consoled her. But Rebecca didn't. She was done with Lily. Lily had finally pushed her away long enough and hard enough to get her just Darien deserts. And because Becca didn't fight for her, she saw the thing she never wanted to see again.

Seeing it, Lily couldn't help but wonder if her ex-friend Rebecca had been right all along. She got up from her tears to chase down the redhead at the elevator bank. Surely Jacob, her Jacob, wouldn't have brought that tramp out here as well. Lilianna saw enough of the body that belonged to the hair to have her suspicions heightened, saw what elevator the redhead got into. She watched and waited to see what floor it stopped at. Another girl stepped up beside her, but Lily paid her no attention. She needed to know if the new Jacob, the soon-to-be-a-Hollywood-star Jacob with Reverend at the helm, was being completely honest with her. The elevator stopped at the fourth floor.

Her hands trembled so bad she nearly missed the button

when she called for another elevator. When it came, she got on alone, though she was sure she had felt someone else waiting with her in the elevator bank. She jabbed the button for four and hoped, prayed to the Goddess, that she was wrong. She wanted to live happily ever after with Jacob...but she needed to know who that girl was.

An eternity of seconds later, the doors opened on the fourth floor. Lily carefully stepped out and peered down the hall in each direction. There was no sign of a redhead or anyone else. Her ears picked up on singing, faint, but not too far, either. The song was familiar, which only made Lily feel worse. It was set to the tune of an old church camp favorite, "Onward Christian Soldiers."

Knowing now, terribly knowing, Lily went towards the singing.

"Onward Christian soldiers...."

The casino hotel hallways turned at odd angles. Up until now, the effect had felt fancy and elite. Now it just frustrated Lily as she closed in on her prey.

"Onward Buddhist priests...."

How could she have been so stupid? What was it about Jacob that made her blind to the dangers?

"Onward Fruits of Islam...."

Maybe it wasn't what she thought. Maybe she was stalking him. Maybe Jacob, her Jacob, didn't know the hussy was here.

"Fight till you're deceased."

She turned a corner and saw her, the redhead with the too-perfect body. She was skipping, deliberate and exaggerated, down the hallway. There was no mistaking her. Lily called the name she had heard from others who had talked to her at the party. "Dizzy!"

The redhead stopped and spun to face her. Joy filled her cheeks, a joy completely unshared by Lilianna. "Lily! Yay! Isn't this fun? We can yell names at each other down a corridor!"

"What are you doing here?" Lily's voice filled with rage, her hands clenching into fists as she advanced.

"Entertaining myself. I get bored staying in one place too long. I swear I've been through every room in this hotel twice and still..." Dizzy was still speaking when Lily swung at her. She dodged with flawless grace and kept talking. "...Jacob wants to stay for the card tournament. I mean, that's okay, that's what she wants him to do, but I wish Jacob didn't want to. Maybe you can talk him out of it."

Lily wanted to hit her,badly, but Dizzy seemed to float effortlessly out of reach. Her anger grew with each missed punch. "Why can't you just leave us alone? We were so happy without you."

That seemed to flatfoot Dizzy, who stopped moving, and caught Lily's next punch in her hand. "I was under the impression Jacob was still happy. I'm very pleased with my skills as a consort... and there's nothing in the rules that says he can't have other wives and fiancées. But I cannot leave him alone, not as long as he is The Hand." Her crimson lips pouted. "Besides, I don't want to. I like my Jakey-poo."

"The Hand of Eris is made-up nonsense. It's a story made up by anarchists on the Internet so that they don't have to pick anyone to be in charge of their made-up religion. All it means is that anybody can be the leader of Discordianism at any given time."

"Oh, really?" Dizzy let go of her fist. "Someone should really tell that to the boss. Boy, I can imagine that conversation now." The redheaded valley girl proceeded to play both sides of it, bouncing between her left and right sides depending on who was talking.

"Dizzy: Boss, did you know you are the figment of the Internet's imagination?

"Eris: Dizzy, what have I told you about reading memes?

"Dizzy: No, no, really, Your High Exalted Chaos-ish-ness. I heard this one from Jacob Darien's fiancée.

"Eris: The one that dumped him and turned lesbian as soon

as the going got tough?

"Dizzy: Yeah, that one, though I've seen her and I think dyke is a bit of a stretch. In the right light, she looks okay.

"Eris: I'll take your word for it. Tell her she can have him back soon enough. I'm getting bored with this whole Vegas gambler routine. He was so much more interesting before you led him there."

At this point in the conversation, Dizzy went from looking stern and solemn while in the Eris position, to panic-stricken when she returned to her own stance. "Boss, no, please don't, he needs you, he'll be interesting again, but he needs to be The Hand just a little bit longer...."

She looked ready to switch stances, but the monologue was cut short by the toe of a boot to her jaw. Dizzy spun past Lilianna and landed crumpled on the carpet behind her. In front of Lily stood the other girl from the elevator lobby. Lily noticed her this time: leather jacket, black steel-toed boots, and long black hair with a lone scarlet bang dangling in front. She was small, even compared to the skinny redhead. The girl locked eyes with Lily. "I take it you know her."

Before Lily could respond, Dizzy dove past her, spearing the new girl in the stomach. Both toppled to the hallway floor, bouncing off both side walls as they landed. Black leggings wrapped around the throat of the redhead. The pair spun and Dizzy was on top, then the stranger, then Dizzy again. Even in heated combat, Dizzy rattled on. "Oh wow, you're really good."

The Gothic assailant had Dizzy in an armbar.

Nothing seemed to shut Dizzy up. "Nice technique, but really...."

Dizzy reversed the grip and it all blurred into red hair versus black, a mist of violently flailing strands. "You're really good, but I think there's been a misunderstanding. Most people have to know me to want to hurt me."

Their heads crashed together, jarring Dizzy's words. "Okay, when I placed that craigslist ad for a new dominatrix this is totally not what I had in mind."

The silent assailant finally silenced her with another solid kick to the head. The raven-haired newcomer stopped to wipe a drop of blood from her lips before looking back at Lily. "You mind coming with me to talk to someone? We've got a few questions and this can be done the easy way or the hard way."

"Umm, who are you? And...." Panic interrupted Lily's reply. "She's getting back up."

Dizzy was on her feet, her head hung low, allowing the mess of hair to cover her face. "Oh, there's a hard way, all right. You picked on the wrong consort." As effortless as a flex, a pair of wings wreathed in flame stretched out behind her. Lily noticed a tiny pair of red horns sprouting up from under Dizzy's hair.

As impossible as the wings, Dizzy's newly clawed hands swung fast. Lily stumbled back as far as she could, collapsing to the floor in her haste. The other girl dodged and danced with a practiced ease. Dizzy was limited by the narrow hallway, her wings dragging on the walls, smoldering and smoking the paint off.

"Fine. You want to play?" The girl's voice, and lack of fear, stopped Dizzy. The girl whipped off her elastic, letting her black ponytail flow free. Her hair dangled to her waist. It should have dangled, by the laws of gravity. But the hair itself started moving. The strands twisted into groups, virtual tentacles, each snaking up the back of the girl's jacket and pulling free a clutch of daggers. The silver metal, black hair, and red fire gleamed and blurred in front of Lily into an impossible mess.

"Demon's blood? See, Goddess, I told you things would get interesting again." Claws smacked against daggers in attack, counterattack, parry. The din and the smoke danced together.

"Call me Goddess all you want. I'm still going to kick your ass." The pair steadily moved away from the downed Lily. Dizzy was potent, but clearly not used to a fair fight.

"I wasn't talking to you." Dizzy turned around and crouched, her wings becoming a virtual tower shield of flame.

The attacker pushed on, her hair unworried by the fire. She stomped her foot onto Dizzy's exposed ankle, and brought a dagger up to her throat. "Game's over."

"Damn it. Good roll, though. We'll have to do it again sometime." With that, Dizzy vanished, leaving only charred walls and smoldering carpet as evidence she had ever been there. Her voice came again, even though her body was gone. "Touch my Jacob, though, and I'll kill you. That's a promise."

The other girl spun about, her ebony tendrils slicing and stabbing at the air around her. All slashes came up empty. Once satisfied that her prey was truly gone, her hair dropped the knives and returned itself to the ponytail position. She snapped the elastic back in place from her wrist and began picking up the fallen weapons. She stared down the hallway at Lily. "Not what I wanted, but at least I'm not going back empty-handed."

Not for the first time since the airplane ticket had arrived at her grandmother's house, Lilianna wondered what she had gotten herself into, but found her brain a million miles away, as if all of this was happening to someone else, not her. She tried to speak, to say something, anything, but words, just like her sense of reality, completely failed her. In her time with Jacob, she had seen some strange things, some undeniable proofs of magic... but whatever had just happened in front of her, between the two women who weren't really just women, was another level of weird.

6

ANDREA

The apartment was dark, even in the middle of the afternoon. The living room windows had been sealed off with heavy blankets, preventing all but the strongest light beams from penetrating. The electricity was off. Even two weeks abandoned, the air reeked of marijuana and other herbal scents less recognizable to Devereaux's nose. She had expected the apartment to look like one of the outer circles of hell. Instead, it looked like an empty apartment, lonely and void. She went back to her car, retrieved her flashlight, and returned to the door marked seven zero two.

The living room consisted of three recliners, two threadbare, gathered loosely around a round glass coffee table. An entertainment center leaned precariously against the opposite wall. Andrea worried that any sudden movement would collapse it into dust. Its shelves bulged down, but whatever heavy load had previously burdened the center was gone now. The rest of the room looked like it had been picked over and packed in a hurry, with plenty of stuff still remaining. A pile of books by the coffee table had been dumped, as if someone had quickly needed one or two tomes and left the rest. The ashtray on the glass surface was full of cigarette butts, some hand-rolled, others factory-packed. A makeshift pipe, rolled out of aluminum foil, lay among them as well. Agent Devereaux carefully picked it up and sniffed at it, expecting the earthy, musky smell of cannabis, but not recognizing the harsher, acidic scent that greeted her. In her time with the FBI, she had smelled a lot of drug aftermath, but she was unable to place that odor.

The kitchen held little in way of clues. An empty box of Little Debbies, a near-empty box of Cinnamon Toast Crunch, and a few discarded wrappers were the only clues as to who lived here. The dishes were all packed away in their cupboard, clean, save for a thin layer of dust. The silverware, on the other hand, lay scattered about the bottom of the sink. She filed it away as a sure sign that the residents ate a lot of takeout and rarely cooked for themselves. The refrigerator was empty, save for what Devereaux thought was a trio of grapefruits under a veneer of green and blue mold.

The hallway closet was empty. Smears of dust suggested that it had been emptied in a hurry as well. The bathroom was likewise clear, save for a cardboard roll stripped bare of toilet paper. In the bathroom cabinets, she found a discarded box for glittering green hair dye and a pair of dirty magazines. Wedged back behind the pipes, Andrea could make out a small cardboard box. The box was damp and its sides tore as she tried to free it, but soon enough she held it in her hands. Inside, she found seven bullets, forty-five caliber. She wasn't immediately familiar with the manufacturer; the rounds were heavy in her hand and might have been homemade. She went back to her car for evidence bags, wondering the entire walk why she hadn't brought them in the first place. With any luck, the lab could turn those bullets into clues.

She stopped as she re-entered the apartment. Andrea Devereaux was a highly skilled, highly trained FBI profiler and her instincts were not to be ignored. Something was different and her gut was bugging her about it. Had she closed the door all the way while she was inside? It had been closed when she went back to her car, but she thought she had left it open for extra light while in the living room. Or was it something else? She was certain something was off with the apartment, but it was more of a creeping sensation on the back of her neck than anything definitive she could identify. Maybe the bullets had unnerved her. Andrea had started to feel sorry for this Jacob Darien, as if he were a victim of an uncaring system, desperate to pay his rent. The bullets, custom-made and of a dangerously large caliber, reminded her that while what happened to him might not have been fair, he was armed and very, very dangerous. She recalled Nicky Alderman's account of the bank robbery in Kingman, and the man who could blow up police cars with his pointed finger, and shuddered.

One of the two bedrooms had been considerably more packed up than the other. What remained was a twin mattress and box spring in one corner. A two-in-one washer-dryer was in the other. Whatever else had been in this room, it was gone now. Andrea sniffed the mattress and thought it smelled faintly feminine and like spilled alcohol.

The other bedroom was more telling. A large queen bed, still dressed in a fine array of sheets, blankets, and pillows, dominated the back half of the room. The window here had been covered with a thick red blanket, painting the room in a dull crimson afternoon light. The blood-like tone jarred against Andrea's nerves as she tried to evaluate the scene. Half the closet was empty, with hangers dangling in place. The other half was all men's clothes: mostly t-shirts, but some dress shirts, slacks, and jeans. The predominant color scheme was unmistakably black. Dirty laundry was scattered about on the floor. Under the bed, she found a green spiral notebook, its cover worn and tattered from heavy usage. She evidence-bagged it and studied the bed more closely before leaving the room, careful to close the door behind her. A man and a woman had shared that room; the woman had taken time to pack her things…the man had not.

Another woman had used the room across the hall. Andrea was reasonably certain they were all adults, particularly based on the arrangement of the recliners in the living room and the utter lack of cutesiness that usually accompanied children. Was one of them the redhead? If so, who was the other? What was their living arrangement? She hoped that studying the notebook she found might give her some insights into this mysterious criminal and his companions. Her reverie of thoughts was interrupted when she tried the front door handle and found it bolted shut.

She calmly set her two evidence bags on top of the crumbling TV stand, freeing up her gun hand. She had not bolted the door. Her hand was nearly to her gun when she heard the voice behind her.

"That won't be necessary, Agent Devereaux. Violence does not become us."

The voice was masculine, an immensely deep baritone, but cracked with age. She turned to face it, trying not to look like she was panicking, but firmly holding on to her gun as she spun. An old black man in worn coveralls sat in one of the three recliners, his fingers folded into a triangle on his lap. Devereaux quickly memorized every detail with a trained eye: deep wrinkles along his eyes, skin so dark it almost blended with the deep shadows.

Her reply was terse. "Who are you and what are you doing here?"

His reply was whimsical, almost melancholy, with a twang of a Georgia accent. "Children these days. So easily startled, so quick to the point." He paused. "You may call me Malachi. Please, sit with me and chat."

Andrea drew her gun from the holster, but kept it at her side. "Let's try that again, Malachi. How about a last name and why you snuck in here?"

"Let's do try it again. Sit."

How she could tell his eye color from across the dark room, she didn't know, but she would have sworn his left eye glowed green like a cat's night shine. The word "sit" was not spoken at her, so much as shot out of a cannon. She could feel its impact, hard like a baseball to her chest. She sat on the floor, unsure of why she was doing it, but unable to do anything else.

Malachi chuckled a little. "You may use one of the chairs if it would be more comfortable. Please, come, let us reason together."

A wave passed over her and Andrea felt like she could stand again. The gun was still in her hand as she made her way over to the recliner furthest from him and sat down. "Who...who are you?"

"I told you, agent, you may call me Malachi. I am not your enemy in this matter." He fished a small flask from a pocket of his janitorial coveralls and took a swig. "May I call you Andrea or would you prefer the formal?"

She nodded weakly. "Why are you here?"

"My reasons are similar to yours. We were both drawn here because of our interest in Jacob Darien. Perhaps this would be easiest if you asked me questions about him, instead of about me and my motives."

"How do you know Mr. Darien?"

"We've never met, at least not in the traditional sense. I know of him, because I pay attention to the rhythms of things: astrology, geomancy, tea leaf reading. He is a very pivotal figure in upcoming events."

She wanted to laugh, to reject all of it as pseudo-science garbage. She didn't. There was something about Malachi and his words that made it all very, very serious. "What events?"

"Are you a Christian, Andrea? Or do you follow some other set of beliefs?"

"I grew up in church, but I wouldn't call myself a believer in anything."

"Non-belief can be dangerous, Andrea. Just because you don't believe in wendigoes doesn't mean one of them can't eat your heart out."

That smacked her. "How do you know about that?"

Malachi smiled, a toothy, almost predatory smile, his teeth glistening white even in the dark apartment. "I told you: I pay attention. It's amazing what you can learn if you pay attention."

The two of them sat in silence for a moment, the smells of the ashtray permeating the air. Andrea risked speaking. "I believe there are things out there. I've seen enough to convince me there are fairies and demons and wizards."

"But you lack a framework for understanding and classifying them. This is an honest approach. It took me a very long time before I was ready to truly be systematic about such things. The classic religions offer many shortcuts to viable understanding, but none of them are true in the sense that they encompass everything. God, in his infinite wisdom, knew that people didn't want or need to understand everything. Some corners of creation are left better unexplored by the masses." He paused for another drink. "Let us assume the Christian framework, then, since you are at least familiar with it from your childhood. You have read of the Armageddon?"

"The battle at the end of time between the forces of good and evil?"

He nodded. "That is how it is described Biblically, yes. In practice, the two sides are not as clear-cut. Granted, Asmodeus and Lilith are not what I would call ideal rulers of Earth, but there are worse outcomes than them winning...My apologies, dear; I can tell by your face I am wandering too far astray from our topic. Jacob Darien is meant to play a key part in the Armageddon. His presence or absence could turn a great many things."

"Is he...is he the devil?"

Malachi laughed. "Heavens, no. Asmodeus is too vain to condescend to a pact himself. He has any number of lieutenants to make deals with mortals. No, Jacob is...he is a keyholder, so to speak. Given the right time and place, Jacob could unlock Armageddon and let it begin...or he could delay it for another century or two. Under the tutelage of someone who pays attention, Jacob Darien could save the world."

Andrea shook her head. "So, what do you want me to do? Stop investigating? Let him go?"

Malachi shook his head. "No, no, you misunderstand. Catch him, lock him up, make him pay for his crimes…but I need him alive." More to himself than to Andrea, he added, "I owe him that much at least."

"That's what I intended to do. I'm not sure we're equipped to imprison whatever he is but…."

"That part, I think, will come easily enough. Jacob is good man, or was once. If you can shake him free from Eris, I think his conscience will surrender him to your justice. But the game is rigged. There are forces that would like to see either Jacob or the Lord Knight or both dead. Plotting for Armageddon is a treacherously unpredictable affair if both of them are in play. They are being thrown against each other, with the powers that be not particularly caring which dies, so long as they are free of one of them."

"Lord Knight? You mean Colin?"

"Hmm. Is that what he calls himself these days? I'm afraid it's been awhile since I caught up with him."

"What do you mean caught up with him? But you didn't know his name?" Andrea's head was spinning, her thoughts becoming thick like the herbal scents in the apartment.

"Dear child, do you suppose that everything that is inside of you is built up in but a single lifetime? Your very bodies are stardust, forged in the supernovas of the brightest stars. How much more your souls are forged by lifetimes of loves and hates." Malachi seemed distant then, sorrowful. "I am only beginning to understand the fullness of that truth and what I gave up."

Andrea could not formulate a question. She was so heavy, so tired.

Malachi pointed to the bagged notebook on the

entertainment center. "Get inside his head, Andrea Devereaux. Get to know him, profile him. If you can get through to Jacob, you can save them both… and potentially the whole world along with them."

7

COLIN

I was ready to call it a night. Building up the kind of cash the targets were after took time, and I hadn't seen any sign of the redhead or her accomplice near the tables. I had enjoyed having drinks with my new friend and I'd like to think I did a small bit of good in cheering her up. She sounded like a good kid who had horrible taste in romantic partners. I did my best to convince her that if someone didn't think she was the best show in town, she deserved better. I headed up to the seventh-story room Veruca and I shared, trying to ignore just how late (or early) in the morning it was.

Living with Veruca and working for Lucien, I liked to think I was ready for anything: assassins, zombie apocalypse, dinner parties with Bill Gates, whatever. I was not ready for what greeted me when I opened the door to our room. A girl in her early twenties, brunette, with a few streaks of green towards the end of her hair, sat duct taped to a chair, with a rolled-up hotel towel gagging her mouth. I stood and stared for a moment, stunned, before absentmindedly shutting the door behind me.

Veruca called out from the bathroom. "Washing my hair. Be out in a second."

When I could find my voice, I was careful to avoid saying

anything I wouldn't want the FBI to hear later. "V? Dear? Who is our guest and why is she...um, here of her own free will? Are you working on our vacation?"

"Don't be silly, Colin. That one's for you. She knows the redhead."

One of the struggles Veruca and I had as a couple was the clash between our senses of morality and ethics. We both had some interesting supernatural abilities and had done things we weren't proud of. But tying up a girl, just because she might know something relevant to what we were investigating, struck me as wrong. I went over to her and started to undo the gag. "I'm going to take this off. Can you please not scream? I'm not going to hurt you."

She looked at me with a mix of heartbreak and fear. "What about her?"

"V won't hurt you. She just gets a little overzealous at times. Can I ask you a few questions?"

"It's about Jacob, isn't it?" Her voice was deep and rich, but still feminine. The undertones of sad emotion laced into her words nearly crushed me.

"Big guy, broad shoulders, scraggly hair down to his shoulders, wears a trench coat. That sound like Jacob?"

She nodded and started crying. I carefully, very carefully, cut her arms and legs free from the duct tape with my chaos blade. "What about the redhead he travels with?"

The question stifled her tears quickly. "Dizzy. He called her Dizzy. She's...I don't know what she is. Fire demon angel thing. Look, can you let me go?"

I nodded. "Of course. But I could use your help."

"Really? You kidnap me, scare me half to flipping death, and you want my help?"

I stayed cool, not matching temper with temper. "I do."

Veruca popped out of the bathroom, wrapped in an oversize white towel. Her hair was soaked, straight, slick, and black, save for the scarlet bang in front, which still looked dry to me. "I do, too. And I ask for it in different ways than he does. So it's up to you whether you want to talk to him or me. I need to finish up my hair."

Her captive flinched at the word "hair", though I wasn't sure why. "Look, really, I can keep her in check. You don't have to talk to either of us." I paused, putting on my best humble helper Merlin look, and hoping she didn't notice my uncanny resemblance to Charles Manson. "My name is Colin. Colin Fisher."

"Lilianna." Her hazel-green eyes drilled into my soul for a long moment. "What has Jacob done?"

"It's a pretty long list. We may have missed a few, but the FBI wants him in connection to a dozen robberies between here and Oklahoma. My boss wants him because he used his robbery winnings to cheat a few of his casinos out of several million dollars. I want him, because the magic he's using is super-level dangerous." Mentioning my connection to the casinos seemed risky, because she might start thinking about gangster movies and leg breakers. But there was something about her that made me suspect she would have known instantly if I tried to lie.

"You know about his magic?"

I moved my head up and down. "I'm a personal wizard for the CEO of a multi-national corporation. Magical problems are my specialty."

"Can you help him? If I talk to you, can you help him or will you hurt him?"

"Hurting is my specialty. Definitely hurting this one."

"Help if I can. He's not going to get to keep the money, but I can probably keep him alive if I get to him first. Tell me how it all started."

She mulled it over and I could see the gears turning behind the mask of her face. "Okay. Okay."

I waited, but nothing more came. "How did you meet Jacob?"

She told her story, slow and deep, her voice weary. "It was

last January. Thirteen months today, actually. We met on an online forum for pagans. I was looking for knowledge, a better understanding of magic…not love. But the first time we met, I knew. I knew that I had been looking for him, almost expecting him, all along. He was my knight in shining armor.

"My background is pretty screwed up. My mom sucked at the job of mother and I never met my dad. Jacob was patient and kind and gentle and… he was able to deal with all the insanity I threw at him and then some. And he…he made sense out of me. I've been diagnosed with every psych disorder under the sun and nobody really seemed to know what was wrong with me. A few days with Jacob and it was all right. I had dissociative identity disorder, the same as him. It happens to a lot of early childhood trauma victims. Brain divides itself into different parts, different personalities to defend itself against the abuse. My own mind made sense to me for the first time, because I could see it mirrored in him.

"Jacob never told me what happened to him, but I know how he got through it. Jacob, Reverend, and David are his three primary identities." My captive stopped. Her face looked like she was selling out her best friend. "Jacob is the white knight, basically: honest, loving, over-protective. Reverend is the all-out pagan: have fun, don't get caught, die trying. David…David is his defense mechanism, the dark, angry one that makes sure he stays safe. He's…intense."

I tried to conjure my best comforting adviser look. "I studied a little psychology while I was in college. I get the idea. It would have to be some pretty grim stuff to impact you both like that. A lot of people have bonded over shared struggles and shared disorders."

"Yeah, well…I loved him, you know. I still do, though…I've put him through worse. I made all kinds of demands on him, trials to prove his love, to convince me he was for real. A road trip here, an apartment there, a new apartment the next week because I wasn't happy with the current one. I know, on some level, I was just trying to push him away. But he stuck. For somebody so completely insane, he's loyal and stubborn.

"Right around Samhain, umm, Halloween for everyone else, he started having trouble sleeping. He would have these vivid nightmares about an hour after he went to bed. They'd shake him up so bad he couldn't sleep the rest of the night. He was still working then, but after a month of that...He couldn't work, you know. I don't know if you've ever been that tired, that exhausted, but he started seeing things when he was awake. He normally had his DID under control, but he started shifting personas randomly without any real awareness of what was going on. He quit his job, because he was paranoid that his supervisor was out to get him and was planning on murdering his grandfather. Random stuff like that, nonsense...But he couldn't sleep more than an hour at a time and he just got crazier and crazier the more sleep-deprived he got."

She stopped and looked at me with a pleading glance. "I'm not sure where we got our money from then till the end. But a couple of weeks ago the eviction notice got posted to our door. Rebecca, my friend, had been crashing at our place. She saw the notice and told me we needed to pack up before they locked us out. We did." Pause. "I'm not proud of that. Jacob saw us packing, said he was going to go fix it. He said he almost had the money, just needed a little more. I didn't know if he would ever come back... there was something about him when he left that was so dark, almost murderous. I waited as long as I could, before Rebecca practically dragged me to my grandmother's house."

I pondered the synchronicity of names, but left it alone. I had a different question. "What did he see? What were his nightmares of?"

She shrugged. "He didn't like to tell me. They bothered him pretty deeply. I don't know if it was the same every time, but one time I got him to tell me. He said there was a giant wolf, a creature of frost and snow, that was ripping people's hearts out of their chests. And a giant tentacled thing made of shadow and darkness that was chasing after it."

I tried not to let that visibly shake me. It was pretty hard acting. I knew perfectly well what Jacob had dreamed of, the nightmare of the wendigo…and the Walker of Shadows.

Veruca saved me by stepping in with a question of her own. "How did you come to Vegas with Jacob?"

Lily nodded, but she seemed distracted by my sudden distance. "There was a party that weekend, at a place we used to hang out at a lot. Rebecca suggested that her and I should go as a couple, flirt around, see what happened. Move on, you know? Jacob showed up, throwing cash around like there was no tomorrow. I hadn't seen him since we left the apartment, hadn't done much except cried, really, and…there he was. Loaded. He must have spent a couple grand on weed and alcohol. And he had that stupid bimbo on his arm. Dizzy. He tried to talk to me, said she was just his consort, a gift, or some nonsense. I didn't really give him the chance to explain.

"That was all I heard from him, until the plane ticket showed up ten days later. One-way trip to Vegas." She sighed. "Maybe I should have stayed home, but I was in love. I came running for him."

I wasn't entirely recovered, but I knew I needed something else from her. "And since you've been here? He's told you why he would have a consort, hasn't he?"

Lily shrunk into the chair, but the answer eventually came. "It's Reverend…his party animal, drug-using, anarchist alter. He got the name because he's uber-spiritual when he's stoned, but his type of religion wouldn't fit in at any church ever. Well, except for one. Temple Discordia…Reverend is the Hand of Eris."

8

COLIN

I stood on our hotel balcony, trying to focus on the case at hand. It wasn't easy. My head felt like it was ready to fly apart at any minute, a wicked migraine in a city that didn't believe in either dark or quiet. Veruca was inside the room, liquoring up our captive, who seemed fairly willing to stay on as our guest at this point. I wished I had hit the sauce a little harder myself. That might have made ignoring my own internal war easier to do.

"You mean the one where this is all your fault?"

"No, the one where this is all your fault, Yog Soggoth, Walker of Shadows, Lord of the Ancient Caverns of Insanity, Master of the Unfathomable Abyss. Your presence, your mere existence in this reality, woke up that wendigo. Then when karma straightened itself out and I killed the wendigoes, you disturbed his dreams. A psychic sensitive, with some pre-existing mental instabilities, gets driven mad because Yog Soggoth is in town thinking about wendigoes."

"Let's keep the facts straight. I killed the wendigo, at least the big one that counted. You accidentally managed to knife a little one in the belly. And you made the pact: one yummy girlfriend for...."

"You don't want to finish that thought. I would never have willingly traded Sarai to you."

"Willing, unwilling, whatever. You said the words and kissed her bloody lips...and no one has ever found her body."

"That's because you spirited her away somewhere. And don't change the subject. You messed with Jacob's brain meats, didn't you?"

*"Look you want to see kingdom come, you got to break a few eggs. If it makes you feel any better, I didn't **willingly** broadcast nightmares at him. It's just something that happens if someone has too close an attachment to the shadowlands and I'm around."*

I was ready to fire back something witty and meaningful when my inner monologue was interrupted by rapping on the glass door behind me. I turned to see a rather sheepish-looking Lilianna. She opened the balcony door just enough of a crack to make herself heard. "Phone call, Mr. Fisher."

The hotel telephone was sitting on one of the bed pillows. I scooped it up, answering it with that memorized pattern from my youth. "Hello, Colin Fisher speaking."

Andrea's voice came back at me. "Colin? Glad I caught you. Are you safe to talk?"

I nodded, then realized she couldn't see my body language. I was a little more drained than I thought I was. "Yeah, I am. I've got some more info for you, too."

"Let me guess. His name is Jacob Darien and this is all about getting enough money to take care of a girl?"

I wasn't surprised that Andrea's investigative skills had been up to the challenge. "I see our lines of inquiry are starting to overlap. The girl who answered the phone is the one he is attached to."

"Good. I can brief you some more once I'm back out there. I've got a few better pictures of him that I can forward on to the Vegas office so they know what they're looking for. There's some weird stuff to report too, but I think it better to wait till we're in person."

"Weird stuff?" I tried to minimize the concern in my voice, but failed.

"The weirdest. You ever run into a guy named Malachi?

Dark skin, acts like he is as old as time itself?"

I pondered it. "Other than the back of the Old Testament, no. I take it you did."

Andrea was quiet for a moment. "Yes, yes I did."

"Name means 'my angel' or 'my messenger' in Hebrew, depending on the context. Could be an alias. What's his involvement?"

The normally stoic, solid FBI agent sounded uncertain, off balance. Or maybe I was hearing too much of my own mental state in her voice. "We'll talk tomorrow when I get there. For now...he wants me to make sure that we don't kill Jacob."

At least, that's what I think she said. The last few words were lost as I rushed to the bathroom, ready to puke.

9

COLIN

When I recovered enough to think, still clutching the cool surface of the porcelain goddess, I muttered some apology to V and Lily and shut the bathroom door. I had been doing too much drinking, self-flagellation, and film noir detective imitations. I had not been doing enough of what I had been hired to do. It was well past time to break out some magic and get myself back in control. I closed the lid on the toilet, grabbed some soap, toilet paper, and the dice out of my pocket. I set everything on the toilet bowl lid and killed the bathroom lights.

It took a minute for my eyes to adjust to the dark, but with a light-sensitive migraine still raging, the little light coming under the bottom of the door was plenty for me to see what I was doing.

"Not a bad plan, kid. Ditch the headache and amp up a magic artifact."

"Quit kissing up. I'm still mad at you."

"Oh, come on, you've known I ate Sarai for years now and you're going to be angry because I accidentally made some guy a few French fries short of a happy meal lose it entirely?"

"No, I'm still plenty angry about Sarai. And the wendigo. I just

figured that was the extent of your damage. I didn't realize we were still a
bleeding fricking blight on the Shadowlands."

"*You win some, you lose some. We're bringing magic back to the*
world, mi amigo."

Debating with him helped distract me from the pain, which
helped me focus on the spell at hand. I crushed up the soap, still
in its wrapper, then carefully poured it onto the toilet bowl lid in
a circle. There was no need for chanting or lyrics to raise up
power: too much magical energy was my primary problem. I
simply genuflected and willed some of the energy from me into
the circle, sparking it to life. Playing fast and loose, I rolled the
dice in the middle of the circle rather than carefully setting them
in place. They came up five and two, a total of seven, making
me think I was on the right track. I rolled the toilet paper into a
tight little wad and focused enough will out of my right palm to
spark the tip of it into flame. I couldn't ignite a car from thirty
feet away like Yog Soggoth could, but watching him do that had
given me enough insight into pyromancy to manage a toilet
paper wick.

I set the improvised candle next to the dice and stared at
them as the fire slowly burned down. With each pulse of the
light, I pushed out from my eyes toward the dice. I thought
about my migraine, my connection to the city, the living magic
of Vegas…and pushed all of that as hard as I could from me to
the dice. At first, it hurt as if my skull were bursting. The more I
pushed, though, the more my head cleared. When the paper was
almost ready to burn out, I just needed to seal the connection
between Vegas and the dice, rather than between Vegas and me.
I did what any Catholic, Rat Pack-loving wizard would do. I
started singing "Luck Be A Lady" to the dice, while still
kneeling in the position of prayer. Just because I looked a little
like Merlin didn't mean I did magic his way.

The spell done, I carefully picked up the dice and examined
them. They had a distinct hum to them, almost like they were
vibrating. I rolled them around my fingers, twiddling over my

middle finger, and under the ring and pinky fingers. Nothing strange happened, no inner light, no overwhelming desire to shoot craps or sell out to the mob. But I could feel the city, the life, the vibrancy pulsing through the dice, instead of trampling through the left side of my temple. I pocketed them, being very, very certain not to put them in the same pocket as my chaos blade, and came out of the bathroom. My head clear, and my guilt temporarily stowed, I was ready to bring this case to a close.

10

JACOB

Dizzy popped into the hotel suite, as suddenly as she had un-popped after the fight with the strange girl. Jacob and Rebecca had been staring daggers at each from across the room, but the arrival of the flamboyant redhead grabbed both their attention. All three spoke at once, a jumble of words with no real understanding. Dizzy's voice was the shrillest and she kept talking after the other two gave up. "So, you see, it's really, really bad, but not like when a chameleon steps in front a rainbow-colored laser bad, more like when a porcupine has dandruff and sneezes level bad. I messed up, just a teeny weeny smidge, kind of my fault, and I'm sure you can fix it...."

Reverend grabbed the reins of Jacob's body and silenced her with a raised palm. "Stop, child, slow down and try again."

"From the beginning or can I start in the middle, because the big-inning was a ways back and I'm really not that much of a baseball fan."

"The relevant middle if thou wilt."

Rebecca jumped in. "What is she doing here? And where on Earth did she come from?"

Dizzy turned to her and stuck her pink tongue out. "Not Earth, silly. Chaos demons come from Hell and the Abyss and all points beyond. Pay attention and try to keep up. And I'm trying to tell you that Lily has been person-napped. It's kind of like kidnapped, except she's really not a kid, so I'm pretty sure it's person-napped, but I guess it could be...."

Reverend tried to interrupt, but David was faster to the mark, shoving Reverend out of the mental cockpit to get to the controls. "Who? Who took her?"

'Umm, David, maybe you should calm down and let me and Revvy-poo talk about this, because you've got a temper and I really don't want to be turned into a toad or flayed alive... well, okay flayed alive might be all right because it would be a new experience, but I would definitely want my skin back when you were done."

David's response was firm and sharp. "*Who*, Dizzy?"

"Um, there was this girl, scrawny little thing, black hair, scarlet bang. Except her hair worked like tentacles, cause I'm pretty sure she had demon's blood in her and we fought, like boom, pow, claws, daggers, fire...it was awesome. Except I lost and she was about half an eyelash from killing me, so I teleported out of there. And when I went back later to look for Lily, she was gone." As Dizzy spoke, a fiery haze of an image appeared beside her, illustrating the girl she fought, as best as she could remember her.

"A demon blood, here? At the peak of my greatness? I'll crush her."

"Look, David about that, you're not exactly peaking. More like downhill slope. Eris is getting bored and when she gets bored she starts looking for a new Hand. Maybe we could leave, go do something totally nuts and unpredictable. That'll impress her and get you back to peak, maybe even better than peak. We could go to the moon or–"

"I'm getting her back, Dizzy."

"But Jakey-Reverend-David, we don't really need–"

David stood and slammed his fist down on the table. Magic flowed off him in waves and the pulse shattered not just the table, but every window and glass in the suite. "I am getting her back."

11

ANDREA

ndrea Devereaux was stuck in Oklahoma City. There was only one nonstop flight per day from OKC to Vegas. The bureau had purchased her ticket for 7:05 the next morning. The bureau would have paid for a hotel room, too, but she found herself entranced by her choice of reading material. She sat in the terminal, stretched out across three seats, sleepy, but unable to stop reading through the notebook she had recovered from Jacob Darien's apartment. Her head hadn't been this muddled since the last time she had been in Oklahoma.

The first page proclaimed it to be "Borderline, Chapter Three". Whether there was a chapter one or two, Andrea didn't know. The handwritten narrative followed the exploits of a young couple on the run from the law for reasons not entirely clear to her. The main character could see auras and seemed to have some understanding of the supernatural. The story would run on for four or five pages and then abruptly stop for a poem or doodling or other randomness. At first, the poems and story made sense to Devereaux. It was dark, but romantic, in a Gothic style. As the notebook continued, the sense of it all became disjointed, random, twisted. The insanity of the author was deepening with each page he wrote.

From a profiler's perspective, the book was an interesting study. Andrea counted four, possibly five, distinct handwriting styles in the book. One of them only appeared in the poetry and appeared more feminine than the others. But across the course of the novella in progress, three of them interchanged practically at random. She would have to run this by one of her friends at the bureau who specialized in handwriting and language analysis, but there was not a doubt left in her mind that Jacob Darien was mentally disturbed.

She wondered about her own mental state as well. The entire search of Darien's apartment was a bit of a blur to her. She could not remember exactly how she found his home in the first place. In retrospect, it seemed more like the old man had called her, summoned her to it, rather than that she had found it on her own. Andrea had seen some strange things in her short association with Colin Fisher, but she had not felt anything like what Malachi did to her. Her conversation with him was fading faster than the rest of her memories and she found herself fighting to hang on to the details of him. Simple details such as his facial structure, hair color, and weight, things that the FBI had beaten into her to remember, were escaping from her as surely as if her skull were suddenly full of holes. When he had spoken, his words had wormed their way inside of her, making her think they were her words, her thoughts, wrapped in his tranquil southern accent. When he had ordered her to sit, she had been helpless to do anything else, but thought nothing strange of it at the time. It was only in retrospect, as his shadow tried to erase itself from her cerebellum, that Andrea began to appreciate just how potent his voice was.

Between the notebook and her thoughts of the old man, whose name escaped her now, sleep seemed unlikely. Add in the man in plain black suit and white button-down shirt who perpetually skulked the edges of her perception, and Agent Devereaux suspected her insomnia to win for a while to come.

12

COLIN

had only been free of Las Vegas's background radiation for a few minutes when I felt a rainbow burst of magical energy a few floors above us. The sensation of sorcerous power flowing free was followed a split second later by a high-pitched scream of glass ripping apart. I started towards the balcony first, in time to see a brief rainshower of shards hailing down through neon reflections.

Veruca grabbed my arm to stop me from going out. "That our boy?"

I nodded. "Unless someone else around here is packing serious magic."

"Take the stairs," she instructed. "I'll take Lily out of here."

"I'm coming with. He may try to track her with magic if he's as stuck on her as it sounds."

Veruca puzzled at me, but kept moving. "But you know he's upstairs?"

"Yeah, and I'd prefer not to fight him inside an expensive hotel with tons of civilians." All three of us were out the door and into the corridor. "If she's with us, I don't think he'll be far behind."

In a weak voice, Lily asked, "Can you keep me safe?"

The question puzzled me, but I stored it away. "Of course. Just stick close to V."

I pushed the elevator button down out of habit. Veruca grabbed my arm and dragged all of us to the stairwell. "Always the stairs, Colin. Elevators are deathtraps."

The flights of stairs went quickly. Seven, six, five. I didn't feel any more outbursts of magic, but my sensation was primarily focused in keeping one foot in front of the other. Four, three, two. Even going down stairs, I found my breathing getting ragged. I was used to controlled bursts and repetition from sparring at home, not continuous cardio. We ran out of the stairwell into the lobby. I was surprised to find the ground floor untouched by our emergency. Down here, they might not have heard the blast. Without the preceding mystic wave as warning, I might not have heard it either.

We slowed from a sprint to a quick walk, trying to pick our way out of the evening crowd toward the exit. Mass panic of everyone running wouldn't help. I needed to get away from this, out in the open. Some place where I could talk to him, reason with him–

"And kick his ass."

"That, too, if needed."

"It's never a bad option to have in your playbook. Speaking of which, the Necronomicon…."

I interrupted him. I knew the book would have helped. But the costs were just too damn high when it came to that cursed tome. As we neared the cashier's cage, I became aware of an unnervingly high number of men and women in plain black suits with white dress shirts. A lot of people got dolled up for the casino, sure. But given my assassin experiences, it felt like I was running past my own execution. If even ten percent of them were hit men, Veruca and I were seriously, horribly outnumbered.

We were almost to the Strip side exit when the first blast echoed behind us. A voice full of rage bellowed after the noise,"

Where is she? Where is *my* Lily? Give her back...."

He punctuated himself with another explosion. "Or I'll tear this whole place down!"

My preference for a quiet discussion away from prying eyes and enemy guns just became irrelevant. I pushed free of Veruca. "Keep going. Get her to the airport. I've got to deal with this."

I didn't wait to see her reaction. I ran back into the casino. It wasn't hard to spot Jacob Darien. He was the one floating a foot off the floor, with electrical sparks twisting around his hands. He slapped in the direction of the craps tables and a lightning bolt ripped from him through the table. Screams accentuated the blast, as people squirmed and crawled away from the ruins.

"No, no, no, no... don't you dare!"

I breathed in, then yelled. "Jacob! Over here!"

"Stupid, stupid hero."

Jacob threw another lightning bolt, ripping through the cashier's cage. I noticed that most of the casino was emptying in a panic. A number of the suits, however, were not running, just watching from a safe distance.

"That can't possibly be necessary."

I shouted. "Over here! I've got Lily!"

"Stupid, stupid, martyr hero."

"Shut up and help me think of a better plan."

The name Lily grabbed his attention. The next blast of lightning was aimed at me. I spun out of the way, but the pulse of energy still sizzled my flesh. He yelled. "Where is she? I want her *now!*"

"Whoa, whoa. Less lightning, more talking. She's a little bit scared right now."

He threw again, this time at my feet. The blast knocked me up and back, bouncing me twice off the marble as I skidded away. "I am the avatar of a Goddess, dark and terrifying, the Hand of Eris. You should all be scared."

I stood up, not entirely certain what was broken or bruised.

"It doesn't need to go like this Jacob. I can help you."

"Help?" He laughed. "Help me? Poor pathetic mortal, all the luck in the world is on my side. Last chance—where is she?"

I had a hand in each pocket, one on my chaos blade, the other on Frank Sinatra's dice. I had been blasted twice and still didn't have a great plan.

"Shield spell. Egg it up, but mean it for once."

I took his meaning and focused my aura into an eggshell around me. It was the first spell I ever learned. It worked great against minor curses or evil eyes. A little under par for lightning bolts, though.

Jacob took my casting as an attack and responded in kind. The lightning bolt hit dead center. It should have killed me, but I could feel Yog Soggoth channeling into my aura defense. The suits were going for their guns, waiting for my transformation. I was sure of it. I needed to end this. Jacob looked startled that I had withstood the blast, but wasted little time in pulling both of his arms back wide. I wasn't going to like what happened if he put them together, pointed at me like a double-barreled lightning gun.

"Luck of an ancient goddess is one thing." I pulled the dice and hurled them at him. "Let's see how well Eris plays in Vegas."

Jacob's hands clapped down together in assault. They closed squarely on top of the thrown relic dice. The resulting bang was the loudest so far, but it was Jacob, not me, and not the casino, that suffered the blow. The concussive force threw him back into the glass walls of the Nobu bar. Then it blew him through those walls, wrecking one of my hangouts. I tried not to think about how much collateral damage we were doing. Valente would foot the bill, right?

The Jacob who pulled himself up out of the wreckage, mercifully not to his floating position, looked different. He was equally pissed, but I seemed to have knocked him down a power level. He growled a threat I couldn't hear. I did see the flash of neon blue, then acid-trip yellow, as a blade sprouted out to full scimitar length in his hand.

I had seen the damage a chaos blade inflicted and had no desire to suffer it myself. I pulled mine and shaped it into a katana with a thought. Now I just had to hope my practice with V paid off.

"And no assassins open fire. Duck back into the elevator bank. I'll take over and we'll end this."

"I've got this. I hope."

Jacob swung wildly as he charged in. I could have ended it, one swift stab. I didn't want to melt him, or petrify him, or whatever "extra" thing my chaos blade would have done. I stepped back, parried him out wider.

"We don't need to do this, Jacob," I said. "Just put your blade away and I'll take you to her."

His brown scimitar became a sky-blue-laced-with-clouds hand axe as he reversed and swung. I stepped back, but he extended it further, longer, sparking off the zipper of my leather jacket. I made a few quick swipes with my katana to force him back on the defense. His anger and size made him strong, but I made use of my training.

"You just want her for yourself. You're jealous. You're all jealous." Tears of rage flowed from his eyes.

"It's not like that, Jacob. I'm just here to stop you from cheating the casinos. I promise: no interest in Lily."

Our blades locked for a moment and we were eye to eye. His were a deep hazel, flecked with gold and ruby. Something about that look stunned me. I had seen those eyes before, knew them from somewhere. The gaze stopped him as well. We knew each other, though I'd be damned if I knew where from. He stepped back, and for a moment, I saw sanity and reason in his face.

It lasted only that moment. He twitched, as if his nerves were being tugged by some unseen internal force. His eyelids fluttered, then opened, filled with a fiery light, as if he was filled with magma.

"Crap. Avatar and a pact host? Eggshell again. NOW!"

Jacob spoke in a deep tongue, a language not spoken on Earth in millennia. "You will not stand against me, abomination!" Powerful waves of magic flowed off of him in a tide stinking of sulfur and rotted flesh.

That was when the ruins of the casino floor began to rattle with gunfire from every corner.

13

VERUCA

Veruca tore her eyes away from her boyfriend as the suits pulled out sub-machine guns from under their jackets. It was easy to separate the tourists from the assassins now: only the assassins were standing. She was out of position and there were too many of them. She quickly worked left to right, throwing daggers aimed for throats. She had no time to watch, to count the bodies as they dropped. She had to trust her skill. Eight targets in and she was on her last knife. There were still a dozen of them concentrating fire on both Colin and Jacob.

V ignored the possibility of Colin's death. She tuned it out, kept killing. She tumbled toward one of the men she had hit. Grabbing his gun, she checked it for a second before strafing at a cluster of six suits still standing. She searched the downed man for another weapon, but found none. A blast of hellfire, unmistakably hellfire, scorched another four of the assailants.

Veruca glanced up in time to see the target, Darien, running away. He was wreathed in crimson flames, taller, darker, than he had been. He was quick, but a trail of greenish balefire dribbled from him as he ran. She translated that to bleeding. One of the assassins ran after him; another moved up to where Colin was crumpled up on the ground. The other loomed above Colin, gun in hand, pointed at Veruca's love. V moved faster than she would have thought possible and tore his throat clear back to the spine in one powerful stroke.

She knelt and searched for Colin's pulse. She felt it, she thought, she hoped, then sped off towards the last gunmen and the retreating wizard-demon-thing. Veruca Wakefield knew the layout of the casino well, but that knowledge didn't seem to matter. Jacob Darien was blasting new doorways, new exits, as he went. At the last hole burnt into the fresh night air, the woman in the nondescript suit paused, thinking the chase over.

Veruca clipped her hard on the back of the head. She glanced into the night, but saw no sign of Jacob Darien. That was all right, though. She had another prize. She checked the female assailant for a pulse and was pleased to find one. Colin wouldn't approve, but Veruca had some very pointed questions for the unconscious woman. She opened the woman's mouth and wiggled a few of her teeth, making sure no hidden suicide pill was concealed inside. She would not let this one die until she knew more about the Faceless and why they were so damn determined to kill her lover.

Checking again to make sure no one was around, she pulled out her unique phone device, a Valente custom build. She called the only number it could call and explained to her boss, as quickly and concisely as possible, what had just happened.

As she stood guard over her captive, she could only hope that someone was tending to Colin. She realized, then, for the first time since before she had joined the military's Cell Thirteen, that she loved another human being. If Colin was dead, if he was dying, people would suffer. Lots of people would suffer, starting with the woman she had captured, and then the escaped wizard. She loved Colin Fisher, but that love burned like violent hate in the heart of Veruca Wakefield.

PART FOUR

INTERNAL AFFAIRS

"People look around themselves and are often saddened by how small their world is. They think that if only they had broader vistas, more opportunities, their lives would be improved. In doing so, they ignore the infinite space that resides inside them: the unimaginable depth and imagination of the subconscious."

- Jadim Cartarssi, Kobold Psychologist and Amateur Freudian

1

VERUCA

The dust had settled in Vegas. Twenty hours ago, according to the Associated Press, a terrorist attack on Caesars Palace had killed twenty-nine and wounded fifty-one others. One of those fifty-one, her boyfriend, lay in the hospital bed across from Veruca. Colin had moved a little, shown signs of life, but had not regained consciousness since the attack. There were things she should be doing, could be doing. People needed to bleed to make this right. Especially Jacob Darien...his blood would make her feel better.

But Lucien's orders to her on the phone had been crystal clear. Veruca was to stay with Colin and ensure his safety until he woke up. It should have been touching to her that Lucien Valente, corporate titan with heart of steel, cared about the safety of her boyfriend. Her anger was still so hot, so eager to leave a trail of bodies in its wake, that she found herself unable to indulge in softer sentiments. Despite this, disobeying Lucien Valente was an idea she disliked even more than the idea of helplessly staying put in Colin's hospital room.

There was a rapping on the hospital door. Veruca looked up to see not a haggard, hurried nurse, but the immaculately put together Lucien Valente. He seemed even more stern and serious than normal. Veruca wondered what he was waiting for. "Mr. Valente? Come in, of course." She stood, vacating the only empty chair in the room. Lucien walked to the foot of the bed at the side opposite her. He said nothing, but stared down at the unconscious form of his personal wizard. Duchess Deluce, reincarnated Marilyn Monroe in the flesh, slunk along behind him and stole her way into what used to be Veruca's chair. Veruca could feel the tendrils of Duchess' mind reaching out, casually invading V's skull. She hated that feeling almost as much as she hated the Faceless and Jacob Darien.

She used the invasion to her advantage and focused her thoughts on the surviving assailant and what she had done with her. A curious look came over Duchess' face as she scanned those thoughts, but she quickly understood and nodded in agreement. Silence held in the room for a long minute before Lucien Valente spoke.

"Your role in this matter is done, Miss Wakefield. When Colin wakes up, you are to escort him back to Boston." His tone did not leave any room for interruption or disagreement. "I have dispatched five corporate response teams to locate and eliminate this other wizard. Mr. Fisher seems to have successfully knocked out whatever was protecting him. We got quite a few useful pictures of him from their battle. Please convey to Mr. Fisher that I am quite satisfied with his performance in all of this."

"Then why are you reining us in? And using five of the six North American teams? Even for a threat of this power level, that seems like overkill."

Lucien shook his head, a subtle but authoritative motion. "There are a number of directions he could have fled. Five will let us cover all bases. And I do not take attacks on members of my Inner Circle lightly."

"Couldn't one of the teams guard Colin while he's in the hospital? My skills are more useful out there in the field."

"I will not risk the most competent personal wizard I have

ever hired further, Miss Wakefield. Even if I wanted to do so, my teams are not the only ones in the field. Cell Thirteen has deployed a squad to find Jacob Darien as well. Whether their orders are shoot to kill, like mine are, or not, I don't know. Five CRTs increases the likelihood that we, not they, get him first."

Veruca understood Lucien's wariness in deploying her. Technically, Cell Thirteen still had a standing order to kill her as a deserter. Under normal circumstances, her affiliation with Lucien Valente kept them at bay, but if they were to run into her out in the field, there could be trouble. She tried not to think about the connection too much, not wanting to give Duchess access to that part of her history, but the smirk on Deluce's face suggested she was failing at keeping her out. "I…I understand, sir."

"I have both an Asian and South American team on standby, should it become apparent which direction they are running." Lucien paused to visually inspect Colin again. "The medical care here seems competent enough, though they were at a loss to explain his condition. Blunt force trauma, Miss Wakefield?"

"He got tossed around by a few lightning bolts and shot. Repeatedly, close range, but with smaller caliber bullets. Not a scratch on him, though, just some nasty bruises." Veruca paused, not wanting to get too emotional, especially not with Duchess still snooping around in her brain. "He had some kind of shielding spell up, I think. Best I can tell it deflected the bullets, but one must have caught him just right in the head, where that big bruise is. Spell saved his life, but he still got knocked out."

Lucien Valente listened carefully to her report. "And the assassins? Do we know why they were on the field of battle to begin with? Or which one of them they were targeting?"

"Seemed like both of them. There was a moment where something…not of this world started pouring itself into the other wizard. That was their cue to open fire…but they definitely were shooting at both of them."

Valente glanced at Duchess and a wordless conversation passed between them to which Veruca was not privileged. After a long minute, Lucien looked back at Veruca, "I see. Miss Wakefield, if you do not mind, I would like to sit with Mr. Fisher for a while. Perhaps you and Miss Deluce would enjoy a chance to eat...or to talk with your new guest."

Veruca smiled. She would sooner slit Duchess' throat than spend quality time with her under normal circumstances. But having a telepath with her while she interrogated the captured assassin could prove very useful. "Of course, sir. Are you sure you don't mind?"

She had meant to ask if he was sure he could protect Colin, if someone tried to hurt him again. Veruca had never seen Lucien Valente fight, or even break a sweat for that matter. Yet there was something so frightening, so intimidating, about her boss, that the question seemed silly even as she formed it. Lucien would protect his wizard...and God help whoever dared to go against him.

2

COLIN

The last thing I remembered was watching the demonic power swelling up in Jacob's eyes and scrambling to charge my own defenses. I wasn't much of a combat wizard, being completely unable to throw a fireball or shoot a lightning bolt, but I felt like I had been holding my own. Then...I didn't remember. Clearly, I wasn't in either Vegas or Kansas anymore.

The room I was in felt very Egyptian. The walls had a color like desert sand and a slight slant inward as they rose. I had not seen anything like it in modern architecture. The walls were covered in tiny pictures, but the characters were intertwined, continuous, unlike the spaced written hieroglyphs I had seen in books. I rose to my feet cautiously, expecting any number of contusions and broken bones, but pain did not seem to be my companion here. My body felt very light, almost weightless.

Another odd feature was that I couldn't hear my dark cobwebby inner voice. He was often quiet or sulking or preoccupied... but I always felt Yog Soggoth lurking in my essence. Wherever I was, I had the feeling he was not, not this time, not this place. In the four years since Sarai disappeared, this was a new freedom for me.

I made my way over to the nearest wall and found it to be

unearthly in a multitude of ways. The surface was holographic. When my eyes focused in on the pictograms, they grew closer, larger, more detailed. The wall did not grow, nor did the room itself, but wherever I turned my attention the pictures revealed their depth of detail. It was overwhelming at first, but when I finally settled on an image, I recognized the scene it was taken from. Engraved in the walls in an ancient style from before the invention of language, there was a representation of Veruca and me at night on the edge of a large feast. I scanned forward on the wall and found it was intertwined with images of men in black body armor hunting down snowy white demon wolves. Tracing backward, I found the scene of me facing off against a lone male wendigo on sacred ground. In epic detail, in the method of human historians from ages past, the wall in front of me detailed my life.

I paused to contemplate what this meant and where I was. I wondered if this was some part or portion of the Akashic Library and if this particular wing was the book of my life. I started to scan forward to the present. I had come to a scene of Rebecca and me talking poolside, when I heard a voice behind me.

"Looking at those walls for the future is dangerous, my love."

I would know that voice anywhere. It haunted me in my dreams, caressed me from my most sacred memories. I muttered to myself, absentmindedly, "Blood of a virgin." I couldn't bring myself to look at her.

Sarai spoke again. "You didn't come here for the future, though, did you, my noble knight?"

I hung my head, trapped between wanting to turn and look…and fearing what I would see. I had dreamed more than once of making love to her with a bloody hole in her chest where her heart used to be. "I don't remember intentionally coming here at all." I paused. "Is it really you, Sarai?"

"In a way. You are choosing to perceive your spirit guide as me. A complete explanation of how that involves the person you know as Sarai would require a deeper understanding of where and when you are." Her voice brought back a host of memories, both good and bad. With each, I could tell intuitively where those memories were embedded in the wall. "You can look at me, Colin. I won't hurt you."

I turned and loved her again instantly. There was no hole, no blood. She looked different, tall and radiant. Her manner of dress was something I had seen in dreams far more pleasant than the others, very ancient Grecian. Her brown hair twisted down in ornate braids before disappearing behind her white toga and olive-skinned shoulder. "Sarai...I've missed you."

"And I you. Though we have never been far, my love. Someday you will understand that, I hope."

I nodded. "I know what you mean, I think." I felt like I needed to confess. "I'm seeing someone. Her name's Veruca. You would have liked her. Similar sense of humor."

"I am aware of your relationships. It does not bother me, though I'm sorry for how it ends."

Another memory of meeting a powerful fairy, The Eye of Winter, came drifting back and I forced myself not to turn and look at the wall. She had told me something then that was so overwhelmingly sad, so full of despair, that I had forgotten her words as soon as she spoke them. "She spoke the truth?"

"From a certain point of view. Colin, the future is always in motion. Prophecy and divination can explore potential lines of being. Believing those prophecies gives them weight, makes those possibilities more likely than they would have been otherwise. Be careful what you choose to believe."

"Then how do you know how it will end with Veruca and me?"

She smiled and it erased any lingering bad memories. "Who's the spirit guide here, Colin, you or me? Try not to dwell on it, my heart of hearts. We are not here to discuss the future, but the past."

My mind returned to Jacob Darien and the odd feeling I had when we had locked eyes. "Where do I know Jacob from? That was what I was thinking about when I…when I….when I was knocked unconscious?"

Sarai nodded. "There is no memory on this wall of that meeting, is there?"

I thought about it, but found no spots in the hieroglyphs of me that called to me when I thought about him, other than our confrontation in the casino. "No, but it was such a strong feeling."

Sarai stepped aside and gestured to the far end of the room. When I had entered, there were four walls, blank save for the murals. Now an archway stood guard over my birth. I tried to see what was on the other side, but it was dark beyond measure.

"You're saying I know him from a past life?"

"You and I have wandered on this Earth for many, many lives, my love. The answer to who Jacob is, to who we are, lies back past many such doorways."

"Take me there, Sarai. Show me."

She shook her head and her image blurred as she did. "You are not deep enough in trance, dear Colin. You came here by accident, but what you seek will require intent. Passing beyond the vanities of the current life is not an easy task. It is made more difficult by just how far back we must go."

I realized then it was not just Sarai that was blurring, but the entire temple of memory. My eyes refused to work, to focus, and the harder I fought, the more clouded my vision became. I felt her lips though, as they brushed across my forehead. "My love goes with you, Colin, till someday and always."

And then it was all gone and I was lost in a sea of pain.

3

LILIANNA

L ily wasn't sure of what to make of her surroundings. She had not had the best luck with men, or people in general, in her life. But she trusted Jacob, loved him in a way that she never would have thought possible. That love, however, was not stopping her from being terrified of him. They drove on through the desert night and he rocked back and forth, back and forth, behind the steering wheel of his old Buick Century. She watched him carefully, out of the corner of her eye, as he carried on a dialogue with himself.

Jacob's rational voice was distressed. "I still don't buy it. There's nowhere safe left on Earth for us."

Reverend chided him. "You must have faith, I say unto you. Morrigan will shelter us. She is a friend of Temple Discordia, even if she is not aware of it yet."

David's approach was far more violent. "We go back and fight. They expect us to flee. We kill the other wizard. Kill all the gunmen he brought with him. Teach them what happens to those that defy us. That should entertain your goddess plenty, right, Rev?"

Reverend shook their mutual head in disbelief. "Eris' love for me overfloweth, despite the Fiery One's warnings to the contrary. Verily, she could not dispose of me for a better Hand regardless of what we do."

Jacob intervened pragmatically. "In case you two weren't paying attention, we got shot. A lot. I've mended them as best I can, but my magic is getting a little unstable."

Lilianna knew the word he wanted to use there and didn't. His magic was getting a little dark. She had seen Jacob do some things before his ascension to whatever his current state was. It had always intrigued her, sparked her curiosity and wonder. But when she watched him healing his wounds, his magic seemed darker, almost hellish. Something worse than Eris was creeping over Jacob, replacing her gentle love with a man who terrified her. "Maybe we could stop, Jacob. The man who caught me, he said he wanted to help you...."

She had started talking to Jacob, but it was David who shot her a dark glance. "Yeah. Helping me was exactly what he was trying to do when he threw those dice grenades at me. Blasted the shit out of me."

"Then Morrigan. Reverend is right. She's good people. She and her husband can help us, I'm sure of it."

Reverend piped up. "See, out of the mouths of babes comes forth the truth."

Jacob replied to himself. "Fine. But we keep a low profile. We've got enough money, even if we did leave half of it back in the hotel room."

Lily watched him, long into the night, until sleep finally overtook her. She wished she knew where everything went wrong. It was only as she drifted off that she realized it had all started to go wrong, really, seriously wrong, the last time she had been in the home of Marianna Morrigan.

4

COLIN

T he first image I recognized when I returned from that distant place was the stern silver-gray form of Lucien Valente, standing next to my bedside. My first instinct was to apologize. "Sorry, sir." I groaned pathetically. "I let him get away."

Lucien smiled. It nearly knocked me out again. My boss smiling was a rare sight. "No need to apologize. You wounded him and chased him out of Las Vegas. That is enough." He paused. "Do I need to fetch a nurse? Are you all right?"

I ran a quick mental inventory. I was sore all over, but no one spot seemed worse than others. I felt like I had a big knot on the left side of my temple, but other than that…. "I'll be all right. I've been roughed up worse." A moment of panic. "Where's Veruca? Lily? Is everyone okay?"

"Miss Wakefield is running a quick errand for me. I insisted she get a bite to eat after a near-24-hour vigil at your bedside. As for the girl, she disappeared after the events at Caesars Palace. My speculation is that she is back with the other wizard."

A knot formed in my stomach. I had promised I would keep her safe. I took those sorts of things very seriously. I tried to push up and out of bed, but found my body only half-cooperated. "I need to get her back."

Lucien restrained me with his hand, but it didn't take much to keep me in the bed. "Mr. Fisher, your services in this matter are done. I have dispatched quite a number of resources to finish off the renegade wizard. I will see that they are instructed to not harm the girl, if it can at all be helped."

"If it's all the same, I'd like to see this one through myself."

He stood firm. "It's not all the same, Mr. Fisher. I rely on your expertise far too much to risk you in open combat. You have unmasked the villain. Men of lesser talent can finish this."

I was too weak to fight him right now. I let it pass. "Thank you for the vote of confidence, sir. Am I still in Vegas?"

"Yes, though I'm curious about where you wandered off to...."

"You are. You have been out for roughly twenty-eight hours now. A bullet grazed your skull... and apparently bounced off without penetrating." The tone of his voice suggested he was amused and intrigued by my apparent bulletproof status.

Twenty-eight hours was a long time. If something bad was going to happen to Lilianna, it might have already happened.

Lucien must have read my thoughts from my facial expression. "Perhaps a distraction is in order. I have need of a way to make people forget a set period of time, typically four to six weeks at a time. Vague recollection is okay, provided they cannot by any means recall full details. It would be better if they could not remember anything at all. Is that something you could accomplish by wizardly arts?"

"I could stick a tentacle in one ear, kind of wipe the slate clean."

"Maybe." I thought about it, ignoring the returned Yog Soggoth's dark whispers. "I would need to check my books on herbalism, but the right brew, properly enchanted, might be able to do it. Can I ask what you need to make them forget?"

Lucien smiled again, this time a more predatory thing. "If I told you, you might invoke your morality clause. Allow me to specify that if you were to succeed in your potion-making, you would be saving their lives. If they remember, I cannot allow them to live. If they can't remember, they could wake up in another town with a few thousand dollars in their pockets. But I cannot allow the contents of their minds to threaten me."

I gulped, uncomfortable with the request, but even more uncomfortable that, if I failed to produce an alternative, the deaths of these unnamed others would be on my conscience. "I think I can. I'll need to get back to Boston to get to work on it."

"I'll see what can be done to speed up your release. I'm sure they'll want to examine you, but perhaps we can bypass any observational period." He started to leave, then stopped and turned back to me. "Leave the other wizard alone, Colin. I am aware you have a stubborn streak. Last time, it gave you that scar to your ear. I do not want there to be a next time."

How he found out about what I did on December 3 was a mystery to me. I hadn't told anyone the full account of that night, largely because I only remembered up until Yog Soggoth took over. I meekly replied, "Yes, sir." Then I added, "Can I ask a favor?"

Lucien listened attentively to what I wanted, then thought about it for a long moment. I was afraid he was going to say no. "Of course, Mr. Fisher. I will try to arrange for it to be there by the time you return to Boston. How much will you need?"

5

VERUCA

Veruca washed her hands with deliberate purpose in the basement mop sink. The maintenance area of the casino may not have been built for their purposes…then again, contemplating the history of Vegas, it might very well have been built for exactly their purpose. The storage room behind her had thick concrete walls and a rather solid door, allowing for all the privacy Duchess, she, and their guest could have wanted. V tried to focus on cleansing her hands, both to make sure she got every drop of blood off and to ritually escape the sins she had just committed.

Love was a funny thing. Veruca Wakefield of a year ago would not have been bothered in the least by a necessary information extraction session with an enemy combatant. Colin's conscience was starting to prove contagious. A conscience was a very dangerous liability in the Inner Circle of Valente International. Better to focus on rubbing her hands raw under the hot water than to allow thoughts to float loose anywhere that Duchess might pick them up.

"It's a shame she was so hollow," Duchess Deluce observed. She had no need for the sink as she had never actually touched their guest, at least not physically. "Whoever programmed her did a rather effective job of scouring her brain meats of anything resembling a history, past, or identity."

Veruca didn't even look up from her hands. "Do you believe her? Did we get everything there was to get?"

Duchess smiled her best amused-goddess smile. "Of course we got everything there was to get. Between your technique and my telepathy, I'm surprised it took us this long to break her. We may have to try this again sometime. Maybe we can go for speed records."

The Faceless assailant had not been able to give up much. For the last two years, she had lived in Chicago. She ran a kiosk on the Navy Pier, slept in a homeless shelter. The suit was the only outfit she owned, the only outfit she needed. Her lifestyle sounded like a miserable mess, but it did not seem to bother her. She did what she did because the man without a face told her this was what she was supposed to do, when he remade her. She came to Las Vegas with two busloads of others because that was what the man without a face wanted. Some were assigned to watch one abomination, some were assigned to watch the other abomination.

Veruca was glad the abomination word was pried out by Duchess and not uttered from the assassin's lips. She was getting a bit testy when it came to Colin and she might have lost control and finished her. Coming from Duchess' lips was all right. She already knew she wanted to kill Duchess. No one called the love of her life an abomination.

She twitched and shivered when a fingernail caressed her back shoulder. Duchess was right behind her. "Any time you want to try, Miss Wakefield. We work better as a team. But if you really want to kill me, I would be happy to reciprocate."

"Get out of my head, fae witch."

Duchess took a step back, just out of leg range for Veruca. "As you wish. So what will you do now?"

Veruca smiled. "Report back to Lucien. What else?"

She could feel Duchess probing at her frontal lobe, trying to uncover her real plans. She could only hope she was guarding them well. She didn't want Lucien to put her on a short leash.

Duchess stared at her intently. "What else, indeed?"

6

COLIN

The next hour was a whirlwind of tests and medication as the medical staff put in the extra effort to make sure I was fit to discharge. It might have been the wee hours of the morning, but when Lucien Valente asked people to do something, they did it. I might have been asleep for more than a day, but I was trending back to exhausted very, very quickly. Lucien had disappeared, likely to go get some sleep, but the echo of his influence was still clearly being felt by the hospital employees.

I expected Veruca to appear at any moment, but she hadn't. Instead, Andrea Devereaux popped in the door as I was finishing getting dressed. My leather jacket looked like it had been fashionably shredded in preparation for a grunge concert. Never mind that I had enough money in the bank to replace it on a daily basis, its condition still made me want to cry. I checked the contents of its pockets to make sure everything was there, then put it on. It would be useless against wind and rain, but it made me feel better to be wearing it.

Andrea's hug hit me more like a tackle. I still wasn't firm on my feet, but she was strong enough to catch us both. "Oh, I'm so sorry, Colin. Are you okay?"

"Pretty sure. You are Agent Andrea Devereaux, right? Not some lake spirit in disguise?"

She pulled back and eyeballed me. "What's that supposed to mean?"

"Nothing. Just hugs aren't our normal greeting."

"I would say you're not normally almost killed, but now that I think about it...Are you really okay?"

"They're letting me go, though I suspect Mr. Valente had to pull some strings to make it happen." I realized I was avoiding her actual question. "I'll be all right."

"Sure, you will. Pact magic regeneration. I'll have you spiffy in a jiffy. After you tell me where you disappeared to earlier. And what that favor from Valente was about."

"Valente is springing you early? I guess he wants you hot after Jacob, huh?"

"He benched me actually. He's sending the trained thugs in to finish the job." That wasn't entirely accurate. I had worked with the Corporate Response Teams before. They were consummate professionals with a lot of experience at making things dead. I wasn't sure how much, if any of that, my FBI friend needed to know.

"Me too. Bosses had me debrief a Major Something-or-Other. I'm not sure I ever caught his last name or what branch of the military he was with, but after Caesars Palace, he's in charge of finding Darien. I'm supposed to file this under weird things I don't talk about and move on."

"Cell Thirteen," I muttered. "Guess that doesn't leave us with much choice. Just head home and let them kill him or get killed trying."

"Yeah, not a whole lot of choice. I've got to get back to Quantico; you need to get back to Boston. No real time to try to finish this."

I raised an eyebrow and regretted it as the knot above my temple yelled at me. "What are you thinking?"

"So, I may have withheld a thing or two out of Darien's

notebook. You know, a long shot, but maybe that's where he's running to, sort of thing. It's in Denver. Of course, you're probably flying out of here."

"You know, I think I read somewhere that if you've been in a coma within the last week you're not supposed to fly. Maybe I should rent a car, drive on back to Boston."

"Maybe you should. Could you drop me off in Virginia on the way?"

I smiled, trying to ignore just how much she did look like the Sarai from my inner temple. "Oh, I think I could find my way to Quantico. Want to have a little stopover in Denver? Nothing work-related, just two friends driving back to where they're supposed to be."

"Why, Colin Fisher, I thought you'd never ask."

Veruca's voice cut in from the hallway. "Really? You're awake for a couple of hours and already forgetting about me?"

"Yes, yes he was."

I shook my head. "No way, V. Though it would probably be better with Valente if you didn't hear that conversation."

Veruca slid up next to me, then kissed me on my cheek. "You're cute, Colin. I won't go out of my way to mention it, but…." She glanced at Andrea. "You better behave yourself. I'd offer to go and chaperone, but then I would be in trouble too once the boss finds out you think his orders are optional. Besides, I've got something in Chicago I need to take care of."

"Chicago?" I was a little shocked. Veruca didn't usually tell me where she was going when she was on the clock. "Anything related to this mess?"

"Nope. Just old business stacking up on my desk." She gave Andrea another look. "Try anything and you'll be new business. We clear?"

Agent Devereaux returned Veruca's glare. "Just business," was what she said, but it came across more like she would like to see her try.

7

LILIANNA

L ily had never met her biological dad. Her biological mom was a piece of work who couldn't keep her own shit together long enough to care, or notice, that she had a daughter or two. Her grandparents had tried to make up the difference with a strict Lutheran upbringing, but by then it had been too little too late. Lilianna had a rebel soul and would sooner die than be a sheep in a flock she didn't believe in. That being said, right about now, she would have given anything to be in catechism class or church choir practice.

She sat, silent, almost stunned, on one of the two well-worn beds in the hotel room. After multiple nights in the luxury suite at Caesars Palace, any motel would have been a step down. This particular one felt closer to eight steps down. Meanwhile, Jacob, her Jacob, sat on the bed opposite her, oblivious to her inner crisis. The demon skank was draped over his shoulder, watching as he checked, cleaned, and prepped gun after gun.

Lily didn't know much about guns, except that she really didn't like them. So far, Jacob had cleaned two smaller guns and a shotgun. He was working on another medium-sized hand gun, his whole concentration on it. She hoped the duffel bag he kept pulling the guns from was empty. Four guns for the three of them already seemed like four guns too many.

Dizzy was talking to him, whispering into his ear. Lily couldn't hear what she was saying, but she knew that face she was making. It was fear and that confused Lilianna all the more. What did a demoness have to fear? And if she was afraid of what was to come, what chance in Hell did she or Jacob have of surviving it?

Lily just sat and watched, traumatized. She wanted Jacob to stop what he was doing and come over to her, comfort her, tell her it would all be okay. At the same time, she thought she might scream if he tried to touch her. Nothing was right in this place. Whenever she thought she was finally used to nothing ever being right in her life, she started to hope that just maybe things would get better. And then the hole got deeper. She wondered if she could grab one of the prepped guns, put it up to her head, quick enough, fast enough, that she could get away with pulling the trigger before the others could stop her. At this point, that seemed a better alternative than continuing in this gradual stepwise descent into Hades.

She felt a hand on her shoulder and spun to look. Behind her stood Jacob, though somehow looking older, more ragged. She looked back to the bed opposite to make sure Jacob was still there. Sure enough, he was still underneath the demoness. She reversed toward the other Jacob, only to find he was gone. Instead, a folded piece of paper sat next to her hand. Nervously, gingerly, she picked it up. She had expected it to vanish away to dust, but it seemed solid enough.

The words on the paper were in Jacob's handwriting. She would have known it anywhere, having seen it in the notebooks they passed back and forth on their dates. He would write and she would write, quick poems to say things their tongues couldn't quite dare to say out loud. It was Jacob's writing on the paper, not Reverend's or David's, clear as a bell.

Someday and Always
I know that it still hurts you,
With too-cheery smiles and toothy false grins,
THEY say that time heals all.
But now still feels like then
And then was several calendars ago.
Maybe you're not doing it right.

Someday, you will be better,
Someday, you will be fixed.
But someday is not today
And today you're wondering if
Someday you might just give up.

I know that it still hurts you,
I know, because it still hurts me too.
And that's okay.
Pain has a way of reminding us
That we're still alive
That the darkness hasn't won yet.

Always I will be here
Not to make you better,
Because I never thought you broken.
Always I have loved you,
Because you always have deserved it.

She read it over, again and again, trying to memorize it, and
tune out everything else that was going on around her. She was
going to make it. She was going to survive this. The darkness
hadn't won yet. When the night grew late and Jacob lay down
on the bed beside her, she snuggled up to him without a second
thought. Someday, somehow, this was all going to be okay.

8

COLIN

I rode in silence until we crossed state lines, first into Arizona, and then quickly again into Utah. I understood that there was nothing magic about state boundaries, but it felt better to be farther away from Vegas, farther away from our betrayal. If this went well, all would be forgiven on the Valente side. At least, I hoped that all would be okay if I could somehow catch Jacob Darien. I wasn't sure what Devereaux was risking with the bureau, but I suspected it would all come out okay for her too, once the suspect was in custody. If this didn't go well, based on my last run-in with Jacob Darien, Andrea and I were probably dead and our bosses' opinions would count for very little in the afterlife. At least, I hoped Valente's pull didn't extend past death.

I saw the sign for Red Cliffs National Conservation Area in the first light of dawn and decided it was probably okay to say something. "So, this lead of yours in Denver? Where are we going?"

Andrea laughed. "You ride with me this far and now you're getting curious? You either have a lot of faith in me or the medication is starting to wear off."

"I'm not a night owl. At least, not anymore. Too many things that go bump in the night. And, yeah, I could probably use another round of pain medication at some point."

"Can you stay off of the pills or do you need another round? If we're going to gain some ground on them, it would help if we could both drive."

I did a brief system check. "I can give up the hard stuff for now, I think. I'll let you know if I'm dying over here."

"Okay." Andrea focused into what I was beginning to think of as her profiler face. "The notebook I found isn't easy reading. Jacob is most likely suffering from dissociative identity disorder and possibly other co-morbid conditions. His thinking got progressively more scattered as the notebook went on. It started out focused on a novel he was writing, with the occasional interruption for a poetry battle, but by the end it was random thoughts, personal journal, and really disjointed creative writing. Given that he can actually throw around lightning bolts, it makes it that much harder to know what's a psychotic break and what's real."

I nodded. I ran into that problem frequently in my own work.

"What if this is all just one big psychotic break? You got hospitalized after your dad died and this has all been one big escapist fantasy?"

He had been like that ever since I woke up in the hospital. He knew I was keeping a secret from him and he would get increasingly more annoying until I spilled the beans and told him what he wanted to know. Except I had no intention of ever, ever telling him where I was while I was in a coma. I needed at least one thing in my life untainted by the tendrils of Yog Soggoth.

When I didn't say anything out loud, Andrea started again. "So Jacob was shoplifting from stores to make ends meet: video games, DVDs, easily pawnable stuff. He'd go out for an hour or two, steal enough to cover bills, sell it all, then go back to the apartment with Lily and Rebecca. He must have been a force of nature at it, because he had their rent covered two days before the end of the month. He's got exactly what he needs, with a little bit to spare for food. He comes home and gets ambushed by Lily and Rebecca who have decided they want a road trip."

I nodded. "Most normal people go, 'no, we can't afford it,' and that would be the end of it. But Jacob is in love and suffering from an insomnia-induced psychotic break?"

"Yep. So eleven o'clock at night they all pack into the car with minimal planning and hit the road. As best I can tell from the notebook, it was the last really happy time all three of them had together as a…whatever the three-person version of a couple is."

I shook my head free of the cobwebs at that. "Wait, all three of them were involved romantically?"

"It's hard to tell for sure. Lily was definitely interested in both of them and I'm deciphering the scribblings of a madman. But it seems like it."

"So all three of them, couple or not, pile into the car and drive. I'm guessing they ended up in Colorado."

"You are right on the money. Turns out Jacob grew up there, not far from your old stomping grounds."

The connections between Jacob and me were starting to pile a little high. I told the universe, silently to myself, that I felt responsible enough for what was happening without any extra added synchronicity. "I really haven't spent much time in Colorado since middle school." Then I shifted attention. "Spent much time studying my file at the FBI?"

She blushed and I tried not to think about how good the blush looked on her in the early morning light. "Hey, at one point you were a prime suspect in multiple murders. I would have been negligent to step into that interrogation room without memorizing everything about you first."

"Flirt, flirt, flirt. Come on, lay it on her. You know you want to."

"Quit trying to get me in trouble. You just want to see Veruca and her go at it."

"You do too, just your version involves less weapons, more kissing."

"I'm going back to ignoring you. I will find the ball gag again."

"A ball gag would fit into your version of events pretty well."

Like I said, when he was trying to get me to reveal something, he could get very annoying.

Andrea waited, somehow aware of my internal distraction. "You sure you're okay?"

"As much as I ever am." I reached over and touched her arm. It was meant to be a friendly, buddy tap sort of thing, but I don't think it played out that way. "So any idea where they went in Denver? It's a pretty big city to just be cruising around in and hoping."

"Hey, some of us have to actually investigate to solve cases. I don't rely on you being able to forge some luck talisman tracker thingy to find him… though that would be useful if you ever want to teach me that one. They spent the night with a witch friend of his and her husband. The husband isn't named, but he refers to the witch as "Mare." Maybe she's just a huge My Little Pony fan, but I'm guessing his crowd is into some darker stuff than that."

I nodded. "Mare is a unique handle. But I doubt it's listed on her birth certificate. How do we find her?"

"Shouldn't be too hard." She pulled a cardboard backing out of her pocket, carefully folded into a tight square. "Back cover of his notebook. I gave the rest of it over to the military guy, but kept this for myself."

She handed it over to me and I unfolded it. On it, in neat feminine script was written:

Marianne Morrigan
10614 Aspen Trail Lane
Lafayette, CO 80026
Ravens_nightmare@hotmail.com
(303) 555-6173
So you can warn me ahead of time next time you're coming! Don't lose this!

I laughed. "Are you sure you don't know magic? Because this is one heckuva rabbit out of a hat."

9

VERUCA

"**W**here did he go, Miss Wakefield? When you told me you were back at the hospital, I assumed it was safe to withdraw my security from him. But now, I see you here, ready to take my private jet to Chicago…with no Mr. Fisher in tow."

Lucien wasn't angry, not yet. He was working himself in that direction, though, and that was something Veruca didn't want to see. Meanwhile, Duchess stood off behind him to his right with a smug smirk on her all-too-perfect face. "Colin didn't want to fly back. He's driving a rental car toward Boston as we speak. And I have a business trip you authorized to Chicago. Easier to cut off the head of the beast than to keep dealing with one claw at a time."

Lucien glanced at Duchess. Veruca knew what he was looking for. Would the telepath nod and agree that V was telling the truth? Or would the slightest shake of her head stretch this conversation out into something ugly? Veruca had been trying, practicing meditation techniques Colin had taught her, in hopes of limiting Duchess' access to her head, but she knew she still had a long way to go in building up her mental defenses. Whatever Duchess ultimately signaled to Lucien, it was so subtle that Veruca missed it.

When he looked back at Veruca, Lucien's silver eyed gaze seemed a little less penetrating. "I assume he has some form of protection with him."

"You saw what he did in the casino on the tapes. You think he needs a twenty-four seven bodyguard?"

This time Veruca thought she saw a slight shake of disagreement from Duchess.

Lucien smiled and it actually made him look more threatening. "I did see. Mr. Fisher is a potent wizard, no doubt about that. But I suspect these assassins specialize in wizard-killing. And you didn't deliberately lie, but you didn't answer my question, either. Which leads me to believe that he does have protection with him, but you would prefer not to tell me who." Lucien processed everything as quickly as he spoke. "The FBI agent…Miss Devereaux, is it?"

"Yes, sir," Veruca confessed.

"Are they pursuing Mr. Darien still? Or are they up to other mischief?"

Veruca focused her internal defenses as best she could, while trying not to look like she was forcing anything. "I think the agent thinks she can turn him into a tool for the FBI. I would kill her if I thought she could succeed." That much was completely true. Veruca had already spent a good amount of time pondering the ways she would kill Andrea Devereaux if and when it became necessary. She hoped the extra truth would overload whatever it was Duchess did when spying on her brain meats.

"Of course. Though…." Lucien paused. "Perhaps I am wasting a prime opportunity by not considering turncoats. Tell me, Veruca, do you think Miss Devereaux would be worth buying?"

"She has certain useful skills. Good intuition." Veruca really didn't like the turn this conversation was taking. She didn't want Colin in danger with her in Chicago…but she didn't like him spending countless hours alone with an FBI agent who looked suspiciously like his late fiancée, either. "I don't think she can be bought. Annoyingly moral."

Valente shook his head in disbelief. "Everyone can be bought, Miss Wakefield. It's just a matter of finding the right currency."

10

COLIN

Desert driving had never been my friend. Back when I both drove and lived out of Dorothy, a 1984 Ford Crown Victoria, it was easy to avoid deserts on the grounds of a suspicious radiator. But my disdain for them ran deeper than that. There was something ominous in the desert. It always felt like something, just beyond the edge of the road, was calling to me, seducing me. There was one time in Arizona, not far from Holbrook, where I nearly fell asleep at the wheel and made it out only because Dorothy's alignment was straight. I had dreams all that night of phantasmal hitchhikers standing on the edge of the sand, staring at me as I drove by. I had been avoiding desert driving on principle ever since.

I wasn't driving and that was part of the problem, too. I was a good long-distance driver. I was an equally lousy long-distance passenger. Without the distraction of concentrating on the road ahead, I could hear the sand's siren song at full blast. Something, just out of sight, just below the mouth of the closest red-mouthed valley cliff, wanted me to come to it. I tried closing my eyes to block it out, but I started seeing ghostly vagabonds with their thumbs out. "Knock it off, will ya?"

"What's up, Colin?" Andrea turned the radio down. "You dreaming?"

"Trying not to, I think." I sat up straighter in my seat. "You mind if I drive for a little bit?"

"Sure. Not sure when we'll find a rest area. Then again, this stretch of road, we could probably just pull over. Any particular reason why?"

"I'm a lousy passenger, I guess. Besides, you look like you could use a nap."

She yawned at being reminded of just how tired she was. "All right."

She pulled over a few hundred yards later at a particularly smooth patch of shoulder. She tossed the keys over to me. "Getting ready to be driving headlong into the sun in another hour. Glad to dodge that detail."

I nodded and pulled a pair of sunglasses from one of my jacket pockets. The move was supposed to be, 'See, I'm a Boy Scout, ready for anything.' Unfortunately, my sunglasses were about as mangled as the jacket itself. One lens popped in two and fell down to the floor mats. "Well, phooey. Maybe I'm not as well-prepared as I thought."

Andrea laughed and I tried to ignore how much I liked the sound of her laugh. I scooped up the halves of the lens and pondered my options. I could have tried to make a pair of shades out of my chaos blade, but I thought the ever-shifting random colors of it would drive me nuts in five minutes flat.

"Or I could fix your glasses."

"That's awfully helpful of you. When did you learn that trick? And why are you offering to help when it doesn't involve your personal gain?"

"Hey, what's the point of being an elder god if you let your human host go sunblind? Can't I just be helpful?"

"The fact that you're asking if you can just be helpful makes me even more suspicious."

"Fine. Burn out your retinas for all I care."

"Well, if you're going to pout about it, let's do it."

I held the remains of my sunglasses in my outstretched palm, waiting for him to provide some ancient incantation for mending things. Andrea was watching, which of course, made it a little cooler. What's the point of having magic if you can't use it to impress FBI agents?

"*Pretty sure you meant to say hot women.*"

"*FBI agents. Now let's make with the magic.*"

"*As you say, mein commandant.*"

I waited for some insight as to how to proceed, but nothing came. Instead, it felt like something was tickling the inside of the palm that held the glasses. Then, the tickling became scratching and pressure. Within seconds, the pressure was radiant pain as a quintet of tiny black tentacles burst through the skin of my hand and wrapped around the broken frames. I think I screamed. I'm not entirely sure, because Andrea's screams were louder and more high-pitched than anything I could have produced.

The frantic pain burned in my hand. The glasses were quickly engulfed by tendrils. It felt like a lemon lined with razor blades was trying to forcibly eject itself from my hand. The world spun and I wished I would black out. I didn't. I stayed awake through a grueling three minutes as the squirming mass wriggled and writhed in my palm. The tentacles retracting should have felt better. It would have, if I hadn't been imagining them racing up the inside of my arm.

When the last tendril uncurled, my sunglasses were whole again. The shades looked a bit darker, almost mirror-sky black. On the sides, a small tentacled emblem in runic shape marked the only major design change. I wasn't sure I could ever bring myself to wear them.

"*There you go. Better than new.*"

"*Bastard.*"

"*You don't know the half of it.*"

Andrea had stopped screaming and was staring at what was left in my hand. "Remind me: I really don't need to see you do magic again."

I shook the cobwebs of pain out of my brain. "It's not

normally that bizarre, just a…."

Whatever I was going to say was lost to the loud rumbling that surrounded us. An earthquake, sudden and brutal, tossed and jostled the rental car. I was still seatbelted in, but got a pretty good throttling. Devereaux was unbuckled and smashed her face hard against the steering wheel.

"There. That should help too, right? Now she won't look as much like Sarai. See, I'm helpful."

The snickers from behind my amygdala reminded me just how badly I wanted to kill Yog Soggoth. *"What's going on? What did you do?"*

"Well, I thought that since you were so afraid of deserts, I might help you overcome your phobia. Work a little shadow magic, send out a nice beacon call to the things that live under the sand."

"You did **what***?"*

"Hey, you gave me permission to fix the glasses. I fixed them. And rang the dinner bell in the shadowlands. Have fun!"

"Unring it. What's coming for us?"

"Tell me what you're up to. The request for the drug from Lucien. Where you went while you were in a coma. Tell me and I'll save you. And Andrea, too."

"I die, you die."

"Only in transition. Otherwise, it's you die, I go back to my exile beyond space and time. I'll find another way back eventually."

"Maybe. The Necronomicon is pretty well hidden back in the apartment. Might be a while before anyone finds it. And Lucien might just warehouse it and forget about it. Raiders of the Lost Ark ending for you, Yog."

"Maybe. You willing to let me kill another one of your girlfriends to find out?"

I hated him then, more than ever. The ground shook again and I could see the earth in the distance moving, as if something large was burrowing underneath it.

"Fine, I'll tell you. Just get rid of them."

"Come on, quick preview first. Clock is ticking."

"I was in a temple of memory, an Akashic record of my life. I could see everything I'd ever done. I could see all kinds of potential futures."

"See, now, was that so bad? Friends don't keep secrets."

"Yog, the ground is still rumbling."

"Fine, fine, back to business. I have the power!"

The tickling, the scratching, started again. That time it was all over my body, not just my palm. Mercifully, I lost consciousness at the beginning of the pressure bursting outward into pain.

11

LILIANNA

She had felt comfortable here, once. Jacob, Rebecca, and she had sat on this very couch four weeks ago. They had smiled, laughed, drank, and smoked pot. All had been right with the world, then. That comfortable feeling was absent tonight, and not just because Dizzy's bony hips were digging into her side.

It wasn't that Jacob wasn't charming. He was at his finest, talking in grand, excited, but vague gestures about the adventures that had brought them back to this house. Sean Morrigan, in particular, seemed to be eating it up, hanging on his every word. Marianne was also having a good time, though her gaze kept wandering from Jacob to Dizzy and Lilianna on the couch. Lily wished she were a telepath: she wanted to scream the truth at them, to tell them all about the dangerous monster that had replaced her fiancé. But she couldn't. Jacob and Dizzy's mouths worked fine, but Lily's might as well have been wired shut.

"And so that, my dear Sean and dearest Mare, is how we have come to seek shelter at your door."

"Legbreakers?" Sean questioned. "See, I knew Vegas was crooked, but I would've thought it would take a lot more than a million-dollar win to get them to crack out the tire irons and baseball bats."

"Well," Jacob replied, eyes twinkling, "Maybe it was two million and I don't want you to overcharge me for the night's room rental."

Sean got up from his lazy boy and clapped him on the back. "No, sir. Not a stinking dime of it. The day I take money from a friend for a bed...." He glanced at the two girls. "It is a bed, right? Or do you need two?"

"One will suffice. Or we can share the master suite if you're feeling particularly generous."

Marianna smiled, but it looked to Lily like the gears were turning behind her bangs and eyes. Her hair was electric blue, long in the back, and shaved on the sides, providing her with an unmistakable appearance. "Not tonight, my dear Jacob. I think you and your companions look too tired for the sort of entertainment Sean might prefer."

Jacob fired back. "Silver-tongued as ever, Mare. No one else can make me feel so good, while still saying no."

"Tosh. Besides, if you wanted the master suite, you should have stayed when we invited you, instead of rushing off to Oklahoma."

Sean interrupted, apparently unaware of the growing tension between Jacob and his wife. "Well, it's all for the best that you're here now. Those mobsters may have done you a favor by running you out of town. Terrible news about the terrorist attack."

Dizzy was quick to interject, finally finding something interesting about the conversation. She had been unusually, eerily quiet, ever since they crossed the mountains into eastern Colorado. "Terrorist attack? Where? Lots of people dead, dying, and twisted?"

To Lily, she sounded genuinely excited about the possibility of carnage and destruction... and unaware that she had played a part in the massacre.

Sean didn't catch her inappropriateness and answered matter-of-factly. "Caesars Palace. They're not sure who is responsible, but most of the media seems to be blaming militant separatist militias. I think nearly a hundred people dead or…."

Lily stopped paying attention to the conversation between Sean and Dizzy. Instead, she was captivated by a subtle dance between Jacob and Marianne.

Jacob started the tango. "You know how it goes. Sometimes you just need a change of scenery for a change of luck."

Marianne sidestepped. "Or before mob justice runs you out on the rails."

Jacob shrugged. "I think the whole trouble with Daniel and Alyssa got blown out of proportion. I'll admit, I wasn't a perfect friend, but really, Mare, mob justice?"

"I was kind to you a month ago, Jacob, not bringing up things I should have. I was just so glad to see you again."

"And I you."

"But…." Marianne struggled for the right words. "You have a history of leaving devastation in your wake." She looked over at Lily. "You've changed out one of your girls. And the other doesn't seem entirely thrilled to be receiving my hospitality again."

"Devastation in my wake? Almost seems tattoo-worthy." Jacob took a knee across from her, while Sean still ogled Dizzy's all-too-perfect demon body. "My apologies if any of the fallout harmed you or yours."

"And that is the danger of your charm. You truly mean that. You would be aghast to know you hurt me or Sean. But if I didn't call it to your attention, if you weren't forced to watch the consequences, you would rationalize it all away and forget about it." Marianne leaned in close, a whisper in Jacob's ear, but Lily could still make it out. "Let the girl go, Jacob. It doesn't take a witch to see she doesn't want to be here. Then, perhaps, Sean and I can help you with this latest tower of smoke in your rearview mirror?"

"It's not that simple, Mare. I can't let her go. I need her. I've done… I did everything for her."

Marianne's smile was sad as she whispered back to him. "The road to Hell is still paved with good intentions, my friend."

12

COLIN

When awareness of the world returned, I was hot. Not just a little hot, but like 'a hard fever deep in my blood burning me up' hot. Whatever Yog Soggoth had done, he'd been nice enough to put my sunglasses on, which dimmed the horrid light that seemed to be coming from everywhere. The desert sand I was crumpled on top of was a perfect reflecting mirror, throwing the sun's rays back at the sky with a fierce vengeance. I tried to shake my head clear of internal trauma and external sand.

Devereaux's body lay a few feet off of me. She was on her back, staring up, bent in an impossible position. Panicked, I rushed over to her and checked for a pulse. She had one, far stronger than I had expected after such a disaster. Her eyes opened as I touched her neck.

Her voice was hoarse, but strong. "Colin? What…what happened?"

"Magic out of control. I'm a little fuzzy on the details myself. Are you okay?" I had expected her nose to be shattered from the earlier earthquake, but no such damage was in evidence.

She thought about it. "Yeah…yes, I'm okay."

With me on top of her, hand on her neck, we stared into each other's eyes. Hers were beautiful, especially without a lake spirit hijacking her vision. We lingered there just a moment too long before things got awkward. I stood up in a hurry, trying to unthink thoughts. "Here, let me help you up."

She refused my hand and forced herself up to her feet. "I've got it. Believe it or not, they teach us big girl things at the FBI, like how to stand up on our own."

There was a bluster in her voice that told me I wasn't the only one trying to reverse an internal process. We spent the next few moments trying to distract ourselves by figuring out where we were. My first task was to look for the car. Not finding it, I went for the easier task of looking for the four lane asphalt highway we had just been driving on. Failing at that, I began to realize that the sparkling new chemistry between Andrea and I was the least of our current problems.

I took off the remnants of my leather jacket, but found that didn't really make a difference in the heat. "Any ideas?"

She fished a cell phone from a pocket, tapped it, then outright slapped it. "No signal. What the hell happened? Last thing I remember…Funny, I don't really remember anything that explains this. You were asking to drive, I think."

At least she didn't remember me going tentacle-beast-from-the-black-lagoon. "Yeah, my memory falls off a few minutes after that. I definitely don't remember leaving the car to go for a desert hike."

"Quick inventory? What do you have on you?" She searched her pockets while removing her sport coat. "I've got my wallet, ID, phone, and my gun. Everything else was in my suitcase."

"Umm. Empty dice case, sunglasses, chaos blade." I dug around in my head for Yog Soggoth. "Eldritch deity from beyond space and time, maybe?"

"Zzz zzz."

"Really, you're sleeping at a time like this?"

"Snores. I handled the heavy lifting. Zzzzz."

"We're going to die out here of heat stroke."

"It's February. You'll figure it out."

Andrea looked at me questioningly. "Eldritch deity?"

"Apparently on nap time. I always thought he was a petulant two-year-old in a Lovecraftian body, but today just proves it. He wanted me to spill the beans on a secret and this was the temper tantrum he threw when I wouldn't."

"My phone has a compass on it. And GPS. Neither seems to be working right now, but we've got to be somewhere in southwestern Utah."

"Yeah, technology and I don't always get along too well."

"So, what do we do? Sun's just about dead overhead, so I'm guessing it's noon. And if I had to guess, that way is south. But where's the nearest sign of life? If we're near the last place I remember, there should be a town north of us. But that's a heck of an assumption that we're still where I think we should be. Cars and roads don't typically vanish."

Was it more of Jacob's phenomenal luck coming to his rescue or was this just the consequence for me letting Yog Soggoth off of his tight leash? I wasn't sure. "It's got to be better than just standing around waiting for something to happen. Why don't we head that way and think while we walk?"

It wasn't easy going. The sand seemed to work against us. For every three steps I took forward, I felt like I was sliding one backward. Soon I was carrying my shirt and my jacket under my arm. I tried to tell myself it wasn't really that hot: only in the eighties, a reasonable February day in the desert. But in my current state, it might as well have been Death Valley in July. Heat–raw, pumping, penetrating heat–and I were not on great speaking terms. For the first time since last December 3, I would have been delighted to have a winter snowstorm.

"Zzz. If you had the Necronomicon you could call up a snowstorm, zzz."

"And if you hadn't lost the car, I wouldn't need to." Pause. *"No*

response, huh?"

"Snores."

"Fine. I'll figure it out on my own."

Andrea was talking but I had missed the start in my reverie. "...doesn't seem right at all. It's too hot."

"Yeah, it is too hot. My brain is starting to stew."

"But what about the where? Do you think we're still in Utah?"

I paused. "But where else could we be?"

Andrea stopped walking to look at me. "We assumed there was an accident and that we couldn't be far from where we both lost consciousness. But look around. There's no red dirt, just sharp yellow sand. And it feels like we've been walking uphill the whole time."

I nodded along. "I stand corrected. My brain is stewed. I should have realized something magic was afoot." To myself, I silently added, *"Especially since my magic was what triggered this mess."*

She looked hopeful. "Do you know where we are?"

"No...not exactly. But I know where we're not. We're not in Utah, at least not on the Earth we're both familiar with. If I had to guess, we crossed over into either the Faerie realm or the Shadowlands." Knowing how we got here, the Shadowlands seemed more likely. But Yog Soggoth had been reluctant to physically carry me into the Shadow before...something about how hard it would be for me to get back.

"Zzzzzz."

"Faerie? Shadowlands? So like another world?"

"Not exactly. There are other worlds, at least, I think so. But Faerie and the Shadowlands are both extensions of our own world. It's not exactly well-understood, at least not anymore. The best I can tell is that there used to be just this world, with creatures of fae and shadow and flesh all inhabiting one space. Something happened, maybe something that got represented in the Bible as the Tower of Babel. Someone didn't want everyone being able to get along, to communicate and work together.

And when everything went south, the worlds split. They all parallel each other, because they used to be one place. And what happens in one has repercussions in the other...but they're not the same place anymore."

I panted my way through the last part of that. I was desperately thirsty. If the heat was affecting Devereaux half as bad as it was getting me, most of that got lost in translation.

She nodded. "Okay. Okay." Pause. "I think I've got it. Sort of. So, how do we cross back?"

"Depends on where we are. If we're in Faerie, we need a ring to cross. I've made circles for crossing back and forth before. If we're in the Shadowlands...we may be in trouble."

"We talking 'remote-control assassin van' level of trouble or 'wizards hurling lightning bolts in crowded vacation spots' level of trouble?" Andrea put a hand to her gun's grip.

"More like 'ice demons eating hearts out of chests' level of trouble. Except the hot side of that, whatever that is." Biblical passages about unclean spirits hovering across dry places danced through my cerebellum.

"Colin, I always have so much fun when I'm with you," she said sarcastically, then softened. "Actually, I do. But is there always something trying to kill you?"

I tried to summon the energy for a shrug and failed. "The exciting life of a personal wizard to a CEO." The rest slipped out before I could think it through. "I enjoy having you around for my disasters."

She smiled. "So...do your thing. Circle us out of here."

"If I try to and we're not where I think we are, we could end up someplace far worse. Unless... think, brain, think....Unless I link my circle here to a known destination. I could target it, instead of just opening a hole straight across to the other side."

"I really don't know what you're talking about, but I'd like to get back to Earth now. Target away."

"But I don't know any circles in Utah or Arizona or...." But I did know one in Denver.

I retrieved my chaos blade from the pocket of my coat and handed coat and shirt to Andrea. "Hold this." I put my hands on her hips and moved her a few feet to the left. "And stand there."

"Right here? Am I allowed to breathe, sir?" Her tone dripped acid.

"Maybe. If you absolutely have to. Now, stay quiet while I 'circle us out of here.'"

I stood with my back to her right side and carefully paced out nine steps as best I could. With my will, the blade became a katana, its icy blue in stark contrast to the surroundings. I put the tip in the sand and began to walk around her in a counterclockwise circle. Normally, I used clockwise for most magical workings, but in this case I needed to banish us and counterclockwise was for getting rid of things. I hoped. My brain was heat-addled, but I needed to trust myself to make this work. A circle is not the easiest thing in the otherworld to walk, but I managed to connect the start to the finish.

The easy work done, I, began to focus on my destination. I hadn't been there in quite a while, not since I had seen the news story about the store changing its name to avoid vandalism. Isis Books was one of my favorite stopping points in Denver, both for books and conversation. Named after the Egyptian goddess of wisdom and peace, it had become a favorite target for drunken idiots who thought the store was connected with terrorism. The bookstore kept one of the side rooms for fortunetelling and other magical workings. I had cast a circle there more than once, back in my wild vagabond days…and I was about to bet my life and Andrea's that I could still link to that room. I tried to remember what it looked like, where everything was, what it felt like… and began to worry that they might have rearranged in the intervening time. Teleporting into a solid object didn't sound like fun.

"Colin, this really isn't a great idea. I mean…."

"Shut up. You had your chance to help."

I genuflected, digging my sword deep into the sand at the close of the circle. I needed wisdom greater than my own. My doubts, my dark cobwebby thoughts, my fears slowly melted away, like the sweat that poured from my brow. This was why I was Catholic: magic, big and vast, was too enormous a responsibility for a human. I needed to believe that something bigger than me, bigger than Yog Soggoth, guided it.

"You mean like your luck spell guided that bus that ran over your clients?"

I ignored him. I had to. As tired as I was, I had one shot at getting this right. I focused on our need to go from here to there. The sights and sounds of the bookstore came flooding back to memory.

"You know that's the room you worked that luck spell in, right?"

Force him down, focus, meditate.

I gathered my will, all that I had, into the blade. Slowly, I began the incantation. "Father, we are strangers in a strange land. Guide us home to the land we belong to. Circle to circle, flesh to flesh, on Earth as it is elsewhere."

It needed to be perfect. I tried to trust the words. "Amen."

I released the energy. My vision exploded in a flash. I heard Andrea yell. Or maybe I was the one who screamed. Geometry, dimension, form became meaningless, obsolete. I was thrown a million miles away and slammed to a stop all in the same instant. Reality fluttered, faded, but I stayed awake. And then it was over.

13

REBECCA AND MALACHI

The Las Vegas Strip was so American, Rebecca thought, but it might as well have been the far side of the moon. Her luggage had all been up in the suite whenever it had… whatever it had done. She had gone up there, ready to pack up and leave. If Lily couldn't love her and give her the respect she deserved, she would go back home and find someone who would. Her self-esteem wasn't so desperately damaged that she would cling to someone who wouldn't cling back. But all that she had found up there was chaos. After Jacob's angry outburst, the entire room looked like it had spontaneously combusted, turning its insides to its outsides.

She had scrounged together enough of an outfit to get dressed after the pool, but finding her wallet, ID, or ticket back home was another story. When she went back down to the casino to look for Lily or Jacob or…really anyone, she was greeted by police tape and a barrage of busy official-looking people. Her eyes took in the carnage, but failed to process any of it for meaning. There were bodies everywhere. She had turned around and sat on the base of the stairs, completely unsure of who she was or what she was doing, until a man in uniform had escorted her outside the building.

Now she stood on the street, not a penny to her name, bathed in the neon lights of Vegas. She had gambled a lot in coming here: gambled that she could keep Lily. She had lost. Worse, she realized that she shouldn't have ever even wanted to win. What good was a friend that was determined to run away from her into the arms of a lunatic? A part of her knew it wasn't that simple, that Jacob and Lily were meant to be, that when he wasn't insane he was a decent human being… but that part of her was still in shock, trying to process everything that was going on. From the chatter around her, she was wondering if she was almost just killed in a terrorist attack.

A black Dodge Charger with deeply tinted windows rolled up to the curb in front of her. The shadow of the tint was so dark that it even seemed to swallow the neon, turning it into dimming swirls disappearing into its depths. A slight buzzing accompanied the rolling down of the window, the parting of the dark veil. An older man, with rich black skin, sat behind the wheel. His voice was deep. "Get in."

Her first thought was that she was now, on top of everything else, being mistaken for a prostitute. She wanted to tell him off, to chew him out, but those two words clawed their way into her mind, quickly killing off all other ideas. She opened the door and slid into the passenger seat. "I'm…I'm not a hooker."

He nodded. "Close the door. Buckle your seat belt."

She did so, even though it seemed so incongruous with her determination not to sleep her way out of her tough spot. "I'm not…where are we going?"

As soon as her belt clicked in, the man put the vehicle into gear and began to show off the power and agility of the American muscle car. There was something beyond strange here, even to Rebecca's damaged psyche. No lights glowed from the dashboard or console. It was the middle of the night, but the man drove, faster and faster, without headlights. There was plenty of light filtering in from the city around them, but he was heading out of town in a hurry. The other cars around them seemed to sense his determination and changed lanes to let him pass.

When they made it past the suburbs, Rebecca could no longer make out the road in front of the car. "Where...why?"

"One at a time, Rebecca. The where is home. I am taking you home."

She nodded, because that made sense. "Okay. I would like to go home."

She could not see him in the darkness, but she could feel him press his hand against her arm. He spoke in soft, deep tones that were almost muffled by the roar of the engine. "I apologize for this, but it will make you feel better. A few snorts will erase your confusion, help you to accept the bad things that have happened to you."

She felt around at his hand and felt a small pouch dangling loosely in his grip. She took it from him and carefully opened it. Inside was a powder, slightly sticky to the touch. Rebecca had been to plenty of parties, had seen a lot, but drugs stronger than alcohol or weed were not her cup of tea. Except this was, because he said it was, and what he said was what mattered. Her brain could not even begin to grasp that circle of logic, but it held fast, despite its oddness. She scooped a little onto one of her fingers and put it to her nostril. One quick, sharp inhale later, the powder burned its way into her nose. Within moments, she felt herself relax, her whole body sink into the comfortable grasp of the car seat. She took the rest of the powder to her other nostril and breathed it in as well.

"Again, I apologize, Rebecca," the driver intoned. "But I must be careful. If Lilith knew what I was up to, it would make everything else that much more difficult, if not impossible."

She smiled, glad that her new friend was talking sense. A warm feeling of peace began to push the confusion from her soul. "Of course," she mumbled. "Must be careful. Don't do drugs with strangers, Mom says."

"Typically sound advice," the driver acknowledged. "But you may have to make friends with strangers and accept what comfort their drugs offer. I need you at a certain place at the right time to lend comfort and aid."

"Comfort and aid," she murmured, now very deep in her seat indeed.

"Forgive me, child. But this sin of mine may prevent many tragedies."

"That's a good thing," Rebecca thought she said, as she passed deep into the reaches of her warm, relaxing mind.

Malachi drove on into the night, determined to make it as far as the Rocky Mountains by sunrise. There were enough cabins, cliffs, and crags there to find safe passage for them through the daylight hours. He found this entire course of action distasteful. It was too active, too hands-on, more than anything else he had done in the past century or two. It was never a good idea to partake of one's own drug supply, but the heroin sounded useful for cutting the edge off his tension. He pulled Rebecca's wrist to his lips and softly bit, drinking only enough to tame his nerves. Even with it in his veins, he flawlessly drove the Charger ever faster and faster, hoping he drove too swiftly for Hell to notice, let alone catch.

14

COLIN

Our arrival caused quite a bit of stir. Downtown Denver in the days since the total legalization of marijuana had seen its fair share of strange things. Half-naked sword-wielding wizards appearing out of thin air in the middle of a bookstore somehow required a stronger word than merely strange, I imagined. Being the said clothing-impaired wizard, I quickly shrunk the chaos blade down to the size of a letter opener and tried to make my parched throat speak.

Agent Devereaux was quicker at opening her mouth and flashing her badge. "FBI business. Nothing to see here." She flashed her credentials around at the various shoppers and clerks. "Move along."

The lady behind the counter pulled a curtain across to separate the bookstore side from the occult area proper, then came scurrying over to us. "Is that…Colin, isn't it?"

I smiled and nodded, panting more than replying. "I'm flattered."

I recognized her, but couldn't put a name to the face. Hers was kind, perhaps a bit too thin and angular to be so easily forgotten. Her looks brought to mind any number of bird species, like cranes and egrets. She started towards me, then got a good look and thought better of it. "Let me get you both a bottle of water. Would that be okay, agent?"

Andrea nodded, put away her badge, and tossed my clothes at me. I took the hint and put on my sweaty white dress shirt, but decided the shredded jacket was still too hot, even with all the holes. I slipped the blade back into the pocket and cradled it under my arm while we waited. The merchant was fast with two bottles of water and a cup of coffee, black with a little cream. I felt even worse for not remembering her name: she knew my favorite drink on a bad, bad day. The darker my mood, the lighter the color of my coffee. The cup looked just right for today's level of messed-up.

We drank quickly, both of the bottles and of the store's air conditioning. The woman waited until we were done gulping before asking any questions. "Should we be expecting other guests via the way you came?"

I shook my head. "I hope not."

Andrea began to eye the area nervously, as if unseen desert assailants might materialize at any moment. "Where are we, anyway?"

The woman patiently replied, "Isis Books and Gifts, dear."

Andrea looked at me. "More fairyland stuff?"

I smirked my best wizardly grin. "Denver, Colorado. A fairyland of its own, I suppose, though, especially if any strange creatures should offer you a hookah pipe."

The clerk nodded. "It's true. Marijuana has changed the state in a number of ways. It's good to see you again, though, Colin. I had thought perhaps we had lost you after the accident."

That wiped the smirk off my face. "Hard to keep a good wizard down. Umm…." I pointed back to where we had first appeared at. "Do you need to know the how and why of what just happened?"

She shook her head. "From the wave of energy that proceeded you, I would say you had a very interesting experience with the fae. But I do not need to know all of your secrets. If it were anyone else, I might be surprised…but I have always suspected you were gifted with a talent beyond most."

I blushed. "A little luck, love, and divination, really. But I appreciate the kind words."

She peered at me hard. "No, Colin. Yours is an amazing gift. You should not discount what you are capable of. I feared I did not praise it enough when you were here before…but there is a darkness about you I did not want to cultivate." I could feel her eyes probing at my aura, studying the pattern of my soul. "You seem healthier now."

That surprised me. Working for Lucien Valente, I generally thought of my soul as being slowly buried under a pile of foul muck. "Thank you. I hope you're right."

Andrea Devereaux, who had once suspected me of murders most vile, chimed in as well. "Working with the FBI, too. He's quite a hero…though I would appreciate it if we could keep our, umm, sudden-appearance gossip to a minimum."

The witch-clerk nodded sagely. "Of course. Not that anyone would believe it if we told them. It is one of magic's greatest challenges and advantages in this modern era: even seeing, people do not see." She escaped her own reverie. "Do you need anything else? More water? A snack?"

I put down the empty coffee cup. "Both? And I'll make the tab right before the end of the day."

That seemed to shock her. "You, with money? Times really do change."

15

LILY

A good night's rest had helped her recover from her shock. She could feel Marianne's hand on her arm, her fingers twitching just enough to wake Lily up. Jacob was up out of bed, of course, standing at the window, legs slightly spread, hands behind his back. It was a David position, she knew, and that somehow comforted her. Perhaps Reverend was losing steam, losing his grip on their body. The thought of Reverend, a man she loved under normal auspices, was enough to shake the pleasantness of a slow waking from her mind. Reverend, right now, terrified her.

Without moving more than needed, she glanced around, taking inventory of the room. Sean and Dizzy were nowhere to be seen, though she vaguely remembered Sean bedding down with them the night before. The chaos demon consort often appeared and disappeared without notice, but Lily was glad she was not there. A black silk curtain, marked with embroidered gold thread in the shape of a complex pentagram, hung above the bed as a replacement headrest. The rest of the room was normal, safe, decorated with fantasy images of unicorns, dragons, and David Bowie. It looked as if a young teenage girl's bedroom had been blown up, amplified, and mingled with a touch of horror and fifty shades of BDSM.

Carefully, she slipped free of Mare's hand. She could feel Ruby coming to the surface, ready to take charge. David would listen to her. The change was accompanied by a twitch of her head and neck. The careful observer might notice her hazel eyes were darker now, flecked with red and gold more than usual. Her voice was calm, authoritative beyond what the rest of her system felt. "My love?"

David nodded, but did not turn. "I am here, Ruby."

She was filled with a desire for his touch, his comfort. Ruby was not a weak creature. She generally considered herself better than most of the masses of humanity; but her David was a titan among men. In him, she could find shelter. She slid up behind him, hands wrapping around his torso. "Are we safe, David? Has the storm passed?"

He tensed and did not answer right away. "I think so. Reverend sleeps, deep and sound. But the nightmares are back."

"The nightmares? Frozen, heartless bodies and a winter wolf?"

He shook his head. "No. These are new. The man from the casino, the one who took you. He is following us. Not as a man, but as a giant tentacled monster. I can feel his approach in my mind. He will not stop until he has consumed me." He paused, his voice recovering its steel. "He is the source of all my troubles, Ruby. He caused this. I know that now."

"But…." Ruby searched her mind, digging for memories that were not hers. "He seemed so kind, so gentle. Are you sure?"

David's nod was tight and tense. "I will be able to rest when he is dead."

She hugged him tightly, wishing she understood, marveling at this thing beyond her comprehension. The others wondered when their fiancé had become so fierce, so dark. Ruby did not. She had known the warrior spirit within him from the beginning. "If it must be so, I will help."

"I know." He relaxed his disciplined pose. "Come. We must make ready for their arrival."

16

COLIN

I didn't envy the task Andrea had taken on of explaining to the rental car company how she, and by extension the FBI, had managed to lose their rental car. I was particularly curious what the car's GPS locator would reveal, if they were able to get a signal from it at all. I hoped it had crossed over into Faerie with us and become a treasure trove for desert gremlins.

"You sure about that? You remember the damage they did to a hotel room with a toy car?"

"I hate it when I agree with you about something."

Normally, in a new town, the first order of business for me was to find a paper map of the city. That's getting harder and harder as the Internet ghostly thingies become more popular. But this was Denver and I didn't feel like I needed a map. Granted, it had been a while, but I grew up here…at least, I did until my mom died. That broke up my dad and me, spiraling me into Boston with Uncle James and Aunt Celia, en route to Harvard. Still, I felt pretty confident in my ability to navigate. Aspen Trail Lane wasn't familiar to me, but I knew the way to Lafayette, and hoped their street naming followed the same conventions as the rest of Denver: alphabetical as you go east to west, numerical as you go north to south.

"It can't hurt that I've got that brimstone scent stuck in my nose. I could track him from miles away."

"Yeah, there's that, too. Can he sense us?"

"Let's assume he can."

I loved Denver. It was one of my favorite cities in the world. But its magic was more relaxed, peaceful. It lacked the raw chaos of Las Vegas' aura. With a cleaner background, it would be hard for Jacob and me to miss each other. He knew I was here, just like I knew where he was. The element of surprise was definitely out.

"Go in tentacles blazing. You've seen his pact form. He hasn't seen ours. Let me out, I teleport us in, we rip him to shreds before he can even build up so much as a puff of smoke."

"It would work. But I promised Lily I would try not to hurt him."

"Fine. I'll gently rip him to shreds. It'll only hurt for a second or ten."

"I want to try to bring him in peacefully one more time. We can talk to him. You can counter his magic, right?"

"Offense is the best defense."

"Yeah, but I give the marching orders around here. Defense will be our best defense."

"Fine. Probably. He's got a lot of juice packed in him from that wannabe deity of his. But I can disrupt him so long as I see it coming."

"And if you don't see it?"

"That's why I'd rather roll in Necronomicon blazing."

I pondered his offer a moment too long, before I remembered what I was supposed to be doing while Andrea…Agent Devereaux…was getting us another rental car. I was finding it harder and harder to think of her as an FBI agent, but that was a dilemma for another time. This wasn't a company matter, but I still wanted my paycheck to show up in my account Friday. I needed to find a payphone.

I won't go into the technical details of why it needed to be a payphone, but like paper maps, those were a dying breed. Still, this was a part of Colfax Avenue that prided itself on being retro. I was sure I could find one if I just kept walking around in the area near Isis Books. I went a little farther than intended and my Catholic guilt kicked in as I walked past one of the adult bookstores. I was pretty open-minded about other people's sexual preferences and habits. My preference had been hardwired to guilty. I blushed at the thought that I might have tried to sneak in there once upon a time as a pre-teen. An odd piece of karma dictated that the first payphone I saw had a direct line of sight to the bright red dirty bookshop.

I used it anyway; beggars can't always be choosers. I picked it up, checked to make sure it had a dial tone, deposited two quarters, and dialed. I hated using this number, but I didn't see a whole lot of other options to make sure I didn't have a CRT team out looking for me.

"Unless they already are and you're leading them right to us."

The line rang three times, then clicked to a staticky silence. I punched in 0710, both my personal code and birth date. It rang once more.

I was quickly greeted by Duchess' silky-smooth voice. "Why, if it isn't the bad boy himself! How are you, Mr. Fisher?"

"In Denver, actually. Doing pretty good other than blushing like a schoolgirl."

"Mmm." Her voice hummed back in my ear. "I do seem to have a talent for that with you. Fortunate, since you seem immune to the rest of my abilities."

"I have nothing but the utmost respect for your skills. Speaking of which…."

Her tone was immediately professional. "What do you need, Mr. Fisher?"

"My wallet got lost in a car accident. Any way you can cancel the debit card and get me a replacement?"

There was only a momentary pause. "Would you like your new wallet in brown or black leather?"

I shook my head, always amazed by her unflappable nature. "It doesn't matter."

A few clicks came through from her end. "I have a bike

messenger ordered and on the way to you. Stay by the phone till it arrives." Another pause. "Is the car accident anything that Mr. Valente should be concerned about?"

"No, umm…." I panicked, not entirely sure of what was okay to say on a public telephone and what wasn't. I had heard all lines in and out of Valente International were under constant wiretap by at least three different alphabet agencies. "The car got lost in the desert?"

Silence greeted me. Then, "Mr. Fisher, every time I think you cannot possibly surprise me again, you manage it. Then it does not relate to your friends in the suits?"

"No. Nope. Just little old me."

"Do you need any more assistance than just a wallet? A new vehicle? Your car shipped to you?"

I almost jumped on that offer. I was missing Dora, my vintage Mustang, something fierce. But given I was about to face off with a guy known for massive property damage, she was probably better off in Boston. "I think the wallet will do. Am I really the bad boy now?"

"You're still in Mr. Valente's good graces, if that's what you mean. He suspects what you're up to, but…" Her voice drifted back towards the sensual alto that always conjured images of her Marilyn Monroe body in my mind. "…your rebel spirit is part of what he admires about you."

"Thank you, Duchess. I'll wait for the messenger." I hung up the phone quickly.

I did learn something else from the call, other than that Valente and I were still good. I would never, ever, ever admit to Duchess that I was blushing again.

17

COLIN

T wo hours later, Andrea and I had wheels again. I paid my long-standing tab with Isis Books, plus a healthy margin, because I liked them. I now had a pink leather wallet with an imitation crystal heart on one side, as a reminder to never tell Duchess I didn't care about color in the future. I also saw a new leather jacket I liked in one of the clothing stores along Colfax and acquired it to replace my shredded one. It still took a second for me to remember that, if I saw something I liked, I could buy it without worrying about starvation or running out of gas. Having been homeless stuck with me, despite what my bank account said.

Andrea was driving towards Lafayette at top speed. I tried giving her directions, but she shushed me in favor of her phone's GPS. Hard to blame her, all things considered. The last time I had participated in driving, the car's GPS signal had ended up in Australia, according to the rental car company. That left me with nothing to do, except get nervous. I could feel him getting closer with each exit we passed.

The trip was tense. I nervously fingered my chaos blade. I thought about every successful spell I had ever cast. And I hoped I was better than the other guy. My nerves just got more frayed. Relying on my combat magic was not exactly where I wanted to be.

The address led us into a section of townhouses. Most of them were newer, another chapter in Rocky Mountain urban sprawl. The GPS worked just fine, despite my presence. It probably figured I wanted it to break and kept working just to spite me. When we were a couple of blocks off of our destination, I elbowed Devereaux. It was meant as a tap to grab attention, but I was wired tight. She jumped behind the wheel and our car swerved.

"What?" she yelled.

"Sorry," I said. "Pull over."

She did so, then nodded. "Right. Car's an easy target and he packs a punch. We'll get the element of surprise."

I agreed, though I knew there was no chance of ambush. I could see him clear as a bell in my mind's eye.

We got out and started making our way towards the address. Devereaux nervously checked her phone, then drew her weapon. I just walked right towards where I knew he was. We were almost there when I felt the shotgun barrel jab into my side.

"You shouldn't have come," her voice said.

I glanced at her. "Lily, look, I promise I won't hurt him...."

"Lily's not here." She whacked me across the shoulders with the gun.

It hurt like hell, but it was an amateur move. Agent Devereaux tackled her before she could point the gun at me again. I could hear their scuffle behind me, but I was focused on the battle ahead. Jacob Darien was closing, and fast.

Still on the ground, I focused my magic. "Jacob, you don't want to do this."

The swagger in his walk told me I was in trouble. "Jacob's not here, either." He punched the ground, his fist vibrating the earth, an instant earthquake. Andrea and Not-Lily tumbled and I fell back flat. "Why are you chasing me?"

"My turn?"

I ignored him and called out. "Because I used to know you."

"Yeah? Was that when you were invading my nightmares?"

He tried to cast a spell. Yog Soggoth slapped it down with authority. "No. You know better. You knew the moment we locked eyes."

"What the fuck is he talking about?" A brief pause. "Verily. There was something in your eyes, my…."

He paused, apparently searching for a word.

I pushed up and kept on. "We knew each other once. Another life, another place."

He nodded. "Thou speakest a riddle, but it hath the ring of truth." The persona I guessed was Reverend wiped his brow, sweat dripping down. "Forgivest my weakness, friend, but I am truly…truly tired."

"I can help you find rest," I said, standing.

"Yes, yes, perhaps you could…so tired. So very…," he said, before a growing fire returned to his eyes. "I don't need your help."

I thrust what energy I had gathered out in front of me like an airbag. Yog Soggoth grabbed it, amplified it, reversing the incoming spell blast. David's hand opened, flashed blue and orange, and threw itself back in a fireball.

"Last chance, Jacob. I can help you." As I spoke, I slowly relaxed my control, loosening the reins on Yog Soggoth without letting go.

David picked himself up. I could feel the demonic energy rising inside of him like an abyssal black cloud. "Have fun, don't get caught, make a pretty corpse."

He threw an acidic green bolt of energy at me. I swatted it away with a tendril, the bolt stinging no worse than a mosquito bite. The me that was an elder deity responded with a spell of its own. A nearby lamppost wrapped around his arms, while the sidewalk swallowed his feet. I tried not to growl out the death threat Yog wanted to speak.

"All too easy."

We started to form a spell somewhere between "knock unconscious" and "eviscerate." My thoughts suddenly slammed shut, my head pounding with an instant migraine.

I heard the voice then, amplified as sound translated to pain. Her voice was a dagger tearing into me. "Sacred covenant, right of land, ban from Earth the unholy blight."

I looked up, my vision blurred, as her spell took hold. In double vision, I saw a slight waif of a girl with a mop of blue hair, but beyond her, over her, radiated a majestic power. I knew this trick in reverse. I was on her land, a sacred space she had magically claimed. There wasn't a whole lot I could do about it. If I had been a normal human, it might not have been so bad. But I was halfway between myself and Yog Soggoth.

A gunshot echoed behind me. Andrea's voice followed behind it. "Ma'am, hands up. Mouth closed."

The witch hesitated, but stopped. Andrea must have been just outside her claimed land.

"Stay…stay where you are, Devereaux. Don't get any closer." I tried to pull myself back together, more me, less ancient eldritch abomination.

"Sorry," the witch said, smirking. "I didn't realize this was official government business."

Her smug tone told me everything I needed to know. I looked over to where I had trapped Jacob Darien. The lamppost still wrapped in a loop, the cement underneath opened up with jagged teeth. But the cage was empty, still sizzling red-hot with a hellish heat, where Jacob Darien used to be.

18

DAVID / NOT QUITE DAVID ANYMORE

The man stood there, staring down at the plaque, contemplating who he was and who he might still be. The whirring, a strange unholy sound, haunted his thoughts, even as it grew and dimmed, grew and dimmed. He was underground. He was sure of that much. The lights here came from strange round tubes in the ceiling, lit from within by some process that seemed like it was once familiar, but now entirely alien. He returned his eyes to the red-bordered, white plaque with black writing on it. He had been the man on the plaque once. He had returned once before, reincarnated by the great Deity, as a man within a man named David. But this rebirth was not like that one. No gentle birth after nine months at rest, he had been spewed full force back into the river of life. There was no rest for the wicked.

The great and hideous whirring grew to a cacophony of metallic shrieks and screams, distracting him. It was deafening, but the metal, the sound of steel flying at high speeds—that was a familiar comfort to him. It made him think of justice, fast, severe, and inflexible. He checked himself over. He was neither young nor old. His clothing was not threadbare, but its design was as bizarre as the lighting: no cuffs, no frills. He wore a suit, tailored to his body, of wine-red material, the color of which made him long for Versailles in spring. White shirt and brown shoes completed the ensemble. It was all so familiar and so foreign at the same time.

He was wondering why he was here at all. He felt like a great failure, though he could not remember any of the battles fought before this. Perhaps this was the state of all undead failures, brought back by some great cosmic force, to stand watch in this new world as sentinels of public safety. He wished the Deity would have provided clearer instructions on what he was to do at his post.

He heard the man sneaking up behind him, but did not particularly care. Why should any man fear who has nothing to lose? Fear, the idea of fear, stuck with him, providing some sense of identity. He felt the blade go up to his neck.

"Give me your money, man. No trouble or you'll regret it." The voice was young, harsh, and scared.

He turned towards his assailant, only slightly, enough to catch his mop of dark hair and a hint of skin. The man did not speak in English, but the newly returned felt like he remembered that tongue, almost as if it had once been part of his name. He shook his head sadly. "I do not think I have anything to give you. I am sorry the world has failed you. The secret of freedom lies in educating people." Even as he said it, he felt like the language, the right language, did not click into place until the last part.

The attacker took a step back, clearly distraught, brandishing the small dagger between them. "What the fuck are you on, man?"

"Death," he said wistfully. "Death is the beginning of immortality."

"Man, just give me your wallet. Threads like that just give me your shit."

He turned to face him in full, not fearing the small blade, for he was already dead, and by a much larger one. "I cannot. That would be an act of pity. But I can...."

The youth stabbed hard and fast, catching him below the rib cage. He looked down, grateful that blood and wine were not so different in color. He still hurt, he still bled, but he held no fear of the wound. He grabbed the teenager's wrist and extracted the blade from his belly. "I can teach you, young man. I can show you the oppressors of humanity, and in punishing them you shall find clemency."

The boy struggled hard, snapping two of his fingers to escape his cold grasp. He fell to the ground, scrambling back away. "Who…who are you?"

"Maximilien Francois…" He stopped. "Max should be sufficient. Will you join me?" He knew his purpose now. The boy had made that clear: an uncaring, unjust society had made him this desperate, dangerous animal. Max had come with a second chance to succeed where he had once failed, to deliver young men like this from the clutches of society.

The boy looked up into his eyes of his would-be deliverer. Whatever he saw there made him try to scream…and fail, finding only unconsciousness as comfort.

Max wiped the boy's knife on his jacket. It was a good knife. The boy was not stout enough to aid his cause, but at least he had provided the start of his arsenal. He spirited it away under his jacket and went looking for stairs out of this underground hell. He would learn what tyrants haunted this dismal world and he would become justice. As a man named David, he had fought for love and lost. Now he would be justice for the oppressed and fear to the oppressors. After over two centuries, the soul of terror had returned to the streets of Paris.

PART FIVE

NEW MAGIC

"I once heard that pity is treason. I'm not sure I believe that.

Someone pitied me once. Perhaps it was a treason for her. But

for me, she purchased my eternal loyalty and devotion. I will

find her again, someday…and woe to the god, demon, or

dragon that stands in my way."

- Jadim Cartarssi, Planeswalker and Lonely Romantic

1

COLIN

L ily sat in the back of Andrea's rental car, hands cuffed
behind her back. Agent Devereaux and I were both
watching her through the glass, twenty feet off. Neither of
us was thrilled with the idea of arresting her for assault or
possession of a stolen shotgun or anything else. But we were
running out of time and options. I didn't know about Andrea,
but I knew I couldn't disobey Lucien forever. At some point, we
would have to stop chasing Jacob Darien. Putting Lilianna in jail
for a few months to cool off might have been a great kindness,
keeping her safe until the Jacob Darien magic show ran its
course.

"I think I know where he's going," Andrea said, solemnly.

I reached out with my feelings. Yog Soggoth was a little
fried from the witch's binding spell, but I still thought I should
be able to feel Jacob's presence if he was near. I couldn't. Either
he was long gone or I was in worse shape than I thought.

"Both? Can't it be both?"

"Big baby. One little binding spell and you fall apart."

To Devereaux, I shook my head. "I don't, Andrea. I'm not
sure I want to."

She nodded. "I get it. It's a tough break anytime the perp

gets away. But I'm in his head."

"Did the witch give you something you could work with? Anything we can arrest her for?"

She shook her head. "Magic without a license? I don't think that one is on the books. Her name is Marianne Morrigan. Claims she doesn't know Jacob. She saw an ancient elder evil on her lawn and felt the need to defend herself and her property."

I am totally sneaking back in the middle of the night and ripping her into tiny, itty, bitty pieces to scatter across the Shadowlands. And then I'll put her back together so I can do it again.

"I get the feeling that, like with the wendigo, the bureau is going to be all too eager to wash its hands of this one."

"I can't disagree with you, Colin. But we can't leave Jacob free and running around to do whatever he wants. He is dangerously powerful."

"So am I. Should I be locked up?"

Andrea stared at me and, in that moment, I knew that she loved me. The pity in her eyes cut into me like daggers. "No, Colin, I wasn't saying…It's different. It's just different. You don't…."

I looked away. "You know me. And you think I'm a good person." I paused, trying not to cry. "Maybe he is too. Maybe we just don't know him."

Andrea put a hand on my shoulder. "I do know you. I know when Jacob was busy ripping up a tourist spot in a magical temper tantrum, you rushed in to stop him. I know when a winter demon was ripping peoples' hearts out, you risked your own life to kill it. You use your magic to help. He uses his because life isn't going his way."

I tried to ignore the tingling sensation I got where she touched me. Sore shoulder, probably. "Okay." I nodded. "Where is he going?"

"Back to where it started. He'll go to his old apartment."

"I trust your judgment. You are a good profiler."

A glimmer of hope sprang in Agent Devereaux's eyes.

"So…up for a road trip to Oklahoma City?"

"No."

"Great, I'll drop her off with…." She stopped in mid-stream, finally processing my answer. "No?"

"I can't go with you. For a lot of reasons. Some of them are easy. Others are not so much."

"Colin…I need you for this. I can't take him down on my own. You've seen what he's capable of."

I shook my head. "Valente needs me back in Boston. But, truthfully, I don't think you need me. If I'm there, Jacob fights. Whatever lives inside of me, whatever lives inside of him, they see each other and it's like two bulls and a red flag. But if you went…on your own…maybe you can talk to him. Reason with him. I think he's ready for this to be over."

She looked me in the eyes. "Are those the easy reasons or the hard ones?"

I stared into her hazel eyes, overwhelmed by just how much she looked like a grown up Sarai. Powerful, hopeful, strong…I kissed her gently on the cheek. "Those are definitely the easy reasons. I'll…I'll see you around, Andrea."

2

LILY

"**A**m I under arrest?" Lily asked. She had been sitting there quietly for a half-hour now. Normally, she assumed that the less she said to the police, the better, but this was feeling less and less "normal" with each passing moment. The female FBI agent had gotten back in the car, put the keys in the ignition, and cranked it up. Then she sat there. And sat there. And sat there.

"Do you want to be?" the agent finally asked in reply. Her voice sounded heavy, like a black mushroom cloud waiting to dump its rain.

"Umm...that depends. What are my options? Can I...just walk away?"

The driver shook her head. "I can turn you over to the local cops. Tell them you attacked a federal agent with a loaded shotgun. You'll spend at least the next five years in prison. And that's if you flirt with your lawyer and the judge."

Lily sighed. "Or? I'm pretty sure I don't like that option."

"You go with me back to Oklahoma City. I'm not sure what I'll need you for just yet. Bait, maybe. Bargaining chip, otherwise. Help me bring in Jacob...safe and sound."

"Do you really think you can?" Lily felt like crying now.

"He's pretty far gone."

The agent sniffled a little and Lily was certain she was crying. "Yeah. But somebody's got to bring him in. Or there's going to be a lot more wrong in the world than one little demolished casino."

"What? But what makes Jacob so special?"

She shook her head. "I don't know. Or can't remember is more like it. But someone told me that saving him was really, really important." She paused. "So what'll it be? Take your chances with the legal system here…or help me save the world from your psychotic boyfriend?"

"When you put it that way…." Lily smiled, surprised that she still had a smile left in her. "I've always wanted to save the world, Miss Agent."

The agent behind the wheel pulled herself together enough to put the car into gear. "Andrea. It's Andrea." She stared off in the direction Colin had walked off in, before finally letting the car move. "Tell me everything. Everything you know about Jacob Darien."

3

COLIN

I walked out of the newly developed community as fast as my legs would carry me. The weather was Colorado perfect: Fifty-eight degrees and sunny, without a hint of storms. A rain shower might have fit my mood better, one of those early summer afternoon thunder squalls that always seemed to flash off the Rocky Mountains. I had to work with what I had though. A little vitamin D might have done me some good. I should have had Andrea drop me off at the airport. But if I had gotten in that car again, I knew, Yog knew, Andrea knew, everybody knew, my next stop would have been Oklahoma City with a possible detour to a steamy night in a Kansas hotel room. Veruca and I... were a thought better saved for another time when my heart wasn't racing with thoughts of Sarai and her Devereaux doppelganger.

My legs burned with a hard ache by the time I reached the first Arvada bus stop. I took my seat alongside an older hippie type. I worried about a contact high from his scent, but I had a lot bigger concerns on my plate. I needed to get back to Boston and get to work on an amnesia potion for Lucien. I was pretty sure I didn't want to know exactly what he was going to use it for, but pondering that seemed safer than thinking too deeply about my romantic life. Did he have top secret research and development scientists working for him who were soon to lose all memory of their big breakthrough? Or would my work be put to even more sinister purposes? I was a reasonably decent herbalist in theory, having read just about every book on the subject in several languages, but my practice had been severely limited by virtue of having lived out of my car for the last three years. Valente's resources had changed all of that, but I needed to find time to work on it.

I was doing the right thing. Right? If I were there, Jacob would want to fight, would feel the need to prove he was stronger than me. I was pretty sure I was correct on that count. But would it be different if Andrea confronted him by herself? I didn't know. I was having a lot of trouble thinking straight when it came to her. Did I love her? Or did she just rile up all my hormones and lust? For that matter, how the hell did I feel about Veruca? I didn't think I loved her in some mystical one-true-love sense…but we definitely had a good time together. It was nice to have someone around who was as fluent in as many languages as I was; definitely expanded movie-night options. But that wasn't a "settle down, get married, have little half-wizard, half-assassin babies" kind of reasoning. Did I think Andrea Devereaux might….

The first indication I had that something was wrong was that the hippie's dreadlocks were lifted up as if fluttering in the breeze…and staying that way. I couldn't feel the wind anymore. Sound vanished. It was as if everything around me was frozen in an instant in time. I immediately imagined a white eggshell around my aura, solidifying the aura with a thought.

"Whoa, whoa, no need for the pointy, slimy, magic stuff." The voice was behind me, close, but not too close. It had a certain valley girl rhythm and tone. "I just want to talk."

I turned around. At the top of the embankment, sitting on a short rock retaining wall, was a girl who looked very suspiciously like Sarai and Andrea. She was a bit thinner, the breasts a bit larger, with fiery red hair and a seductive smile. It was attractive and repulsive at the same time, like a caricature of the real thing. Her clothing…I tried not to pay much attention to what little there was of it. I pumped whatever hormonal energy that arose into my dragonshell defense spell.

"You like it, right?" She stood up to show off what would normally have been considered a very nice pair of legs. "I kind of have a talent for knowing just what people like to see. Feel free to comment if I didn't get it right. I can be very…flexible." She drew out the word so long and sharp it could have been a weapon.

"Not to be rude, but I'm not in the mood for it. If you want to talk…."

She interrupted. "Are you sure you're not in the mood? Awfully hard to lie to a succubus-blooded chaos demon. We've got a sixth sense for this sort of thing. Think of me as a freebie. You get to do *whatever*." That word was emphasized to the size of a freight train. "And you don't need to worry about your girlfriend ever finding out or the other girl getting hurt. Time freeze is real useful for that. It's also useful for watching a sunset, except the sun never really sets, but it's still so romantic."

"You seem to know a lot about me. And I think I know you by reputation. You are Dizzy, consort to Jacob Darien."

She shrugged and I thought I saw a brief flash of sorrow across her face. "Consort to the Hand of Eris, whoever happens to hold that title. It's more like being the pass-around girl for a biker gang. Ooo…that kind of sounds like fun. Maybe…."

"What do you want, Dizzy? And can you please look like someone else?"

"Are you sure, Colin? I could do things for you that Veruca can't even…." She stopped, held fast by the death glare I was sending. "Oh, all right. Stick in the mud." She shifted back to something closer to the reports we had in Vegas, complete with sleek, sequined red dress with high leg slit. "Better? You mortals get so weird when you're in love."

I caught something in the way her face changed as she said "in love," a micro-expression that could have been very telling had I known anything about her. "Thank you, Dizzy. Is this a formal negotiation on behalf of your master?"

She shook her head and started crying. "No."

Maybe it was another trick in the seductive succubus playbook, but I fell for it hook, line, and sinker. Tears were not my strong suit. I dropped my defenses and closed the distance between us. "What can I do for you, Dizzy?"

"I'd like to offer a trade. My services for yours." She sniveled through her tears. "I want…I want you to banish me."

"Banish you? Permanently?" I was astonished. If my guard could have dropped any lower, it would have.

"It usually takes hold for a year and a day. I've heard of different banishment effects… but I don't want to be here right now. If I can be here, she'll make me be here, make me do things…and I'd rather just sit and cry in Hell and eat some ice cream." She started bawling in earnest. "Why don't we have ice cream in Hell? Why?"

I put my arms around her and pulled her into my chest, letting her cry it out on my shoulder. She was warm to the touch. The contact made my blood race, amplifying my thoughts about both Veruca and Andrea a hundredfold. I don't think she did it on purpose…just an effect her kind had on mortal men. I tried to tune it out. "I'll banish you."

She cried some more, her tears hot, almost burning on my chest. "It's…it's got to be…got to be a fair trade. Otherwise…she'll know I let you…let you banish me."

"Who? Who would know?"

She stopped crying and looked up at me with large desperate eyes, chewing on her own lips. She shook her head as if begging me not to ask that question again.

"Okay. So what can you offer in trade?"

She stood up on her tippy toes and whispered into my ear. The notes were so erotic, each syllable so laced with lust, I stopped paying attention to what she actually said.

I shook my head, glad for once that my Catholic sense of guilt and fear of demonic entanglements was strongly imprinted. "Not that, Dizzy. I...I can't do anything sexual with you."

She smiled a little, a sad smile. "First man in a thousand years to pass." She nodded. "Your love is lucky to have you."

I laughed in frustration. "Just wish I knew who it was I loved."

She put a hand on my cheek. "You'll figure it out." She looked around us. "So...what are you waiting on the bus for? Don't you wizards like...I don't know...teleport or drive really cool cars. Jacob...." She stopped and this time I was certain it was heartbreak in her eyes.

"I missed teleportation day in wizard school." I thought back to the Faerie Desert. "Well, mostly."

"Where are you going?" she asked. "I could get you there so fast it would make your head spin. One teleport for one banishing spell. Is that a fair trade?"

I nodded. "Can you tell me what happened with Jacob?"

"I don't know. It's like he broke. He put together a spell to run, to teleport away... and something went wrong. David went one way, Jacob went another...and Reverend... Reverend's not the Hand of Eris anymore." She started bawling again.

I just held her and let her cry it out.

4

VERUCA

S he sat perched on the corner of the rooftop, watching the small white building across the street from her. For an ice cream shop two blocks from Chicago's Union Station, they sure didn't have a lot of customers going in and out. She had seen enough people come out with shakes or sundaes to be sure that they did sell ice cream, but she was very certain the business did quite a bit more than that. Men and women in cheap black suits and white dress shirts seemed to come and go like clockwork, walking fast and with purpose as they went in, and leaving considerably calmer when they shambled out. They all looked so alike that Veruca was having trouble being sure how long they stayed in there, but her best guess was forty-five minutes to an hour.

She wished she wasn't in such a damn hurry. Normally, Valente International company resources had her hits carefully mapped out before she ever got the call. But all six CRT teams in North America were currently deployed and most of the company's other covert options were busy researching rogue wizards. That left her to do both reconnaissance and execution on the target. She had experience at recon, but this was turning into a very complex target for one little assassin.

She had picked up the scent on Navy Pier. Like her guest in

the Vegas basement had said, there were a number of the Faceless agents running kiosks on the pier during the day and evening, before heading off to a homeless shelter or a back alley for the night. When they woke, they each went through a morning stretch and workout routine that looked very Middle Eastern to her eye, something similar to Krav Maga, but not identical. They had no contact with each other, no common point of intersection that Veruca could find...except for the ice cream shop. Once a day, each would individually close up his or her kiosk and take a walk to the store below. Their departures appeared to be timed about a half-hour apart, continuously through the afternoon and evening.

If she had to guess, the ice cream shop was a front for maintaining whatever programming had been used to hollow them out into kiosk-running killing machines. They would come in once per day, hand over the profits from their kiosk, and then get re-upped. From the way they staggered on their way out, Veruca suspected they were using heroin as part of the indoctrination. The martial arts and drug of choice made her think the real base of operation was a long way away from the busy heart of Chicago. She had two options: she could watch from up here for another two or three days and maybe, maybe, pick out a few of the higher-ups. Or she could follow in one of the suits by thirty seconds and see where they went once they were inside.

The second route would most likely get bloody and fast, even if there were no customers. She hadn't seen any civilians go in during the last half-hour. A great assassin would have picked the first route. Veruca had washed out of Cell Thirteen for being too impulsive and she didn't see any reason to start playing things differently now.

She clambered down the fire escape to the alley behind her building and picked a good vantage point to watch for the next suit to wander in from the pier. Her wait was short, only a few minutes, before she saw one walking a hurried agitated walk towards the storefront. She checked her daggers with one hand, almost subconsciously, before crossing the street towards the now-open glass door. She slid in just as it was about to shut, trying to avoid ringing the bell. A young teenage boy with a faceful of frightful acne stood behind the counter, polishing the brightwork, face down, not noticing her. The suit had his hand on a door between the men's room and the ladies' room, twisting the handle in the opposite of expected directions.

Veruca silently slipped up behind the soda jerk and put him down with a quick chop to the side of his jaw. She tucked the body behind the counter. He would wake up, eventually, but with a heck of a bruise. She jumped the freezers and headed back to where the suit had been. The door was shut, but it opened for her when she lifted the handle. Dark stairs led down below. Her demon-blooded eyes quickly picked up enough detail to descend. She moved as quietly as she could, drawing one dagger from her stored clutch. She doubted there were civilians past this point.

The room below was small and bare. Two women in suits were splayed out on the floor, one sleeve on each rolled up past the elbow. The man she had followed was handing a bank bag to another man in a carved ivory mask. The suit man was focused on the masked man. The masked man was not and saw her enter. He dropped what he was holding, reaching down underneath the podium he stood behind. Veruca sprang, her dagger flying at the inattentive standing suit. She would have liked to have gone for the mask, but she needed him alive. She already knew what suits knew.

She rolled across the first woman on the floor with a quick stab, as the masked man opened fire. Not even glancing, she recognized the discharge of a Desert Eagle when she heard one. Powerful weapon, but not easy to aim quickly between shots. She spun back, throwing the second dagger at the other woman instead of stabbing her directly. The second gunshot failed to predict Veruca, nearly taking the head off the dozing suit woman. With reflexes not natural to humans, Veruca closed the distance between her and the gunman. Her ponytail wrapped around his hands, jerking the third and final shot wide. She rose with a decisive kick to his groin. Standing, she kicked away his gun, then his mask. The face underneath was in pain, but recovering to anger. She stomped her combat boot on the side of his head. He went limp.

The action ended, she quickly checked the three suits to make sure they were dead. The woman she had stabbed was not and Veruca quickly sent her on her way to whatever afterlife there was. One steel door next to the podium led out, the only exit beyond the way she entered. She hesitated between pushing her luck and being satisfied with her take for the day. Veruca Wakefield of a year ago would have gone past the door, chased how deep the rabbit hole went. Maybe she was becoming a better assassin…or maybe she wanted to take what little she had and process it into information Valente could use to protect her favorite wizard.

She cleaned out nearly two dozen bank bags from under the podium into a backpack half full of syringes and white powder. She forced the mask on top, zipped it up, and slipped it over her shoulders. She dragged the unconscious man, who maskless looked very Arabic to her, up the stairs, and deposited him behind the counter with the out-cold ice cream vendor. She looked at the store's telephone, debating the risks, before using it to dial an emergency number to Duchess Deluce. This was not the cleanest operation in the world, but there was less risk calling from here than dragging her captive out on to the busy streets of Chicago.

5

ANDREA

A ndrea Devereaux, rogue FBI agent, gave up and checked
into the Salina, Kansas Best Western. She was eager to see
this thing to conclusion, but exhaustion was taking over. It
had been a long, long time since she had slept. Her prisoner/co-
conspirator had been sleeping in the back seat. She had uncuffed
Lily when they stopped for gas in Burlington. Her profiler gut
told her that Lily was genuinely cooperating with her. They
wanted the same thing, mostly: Jacob Darien alive and free from
whatever disaster he had created for himself. She helped her up
to their room and by the time they reached room 317, they were
both leaning on each other like two heavyweight boxers in a
double-digit round of a match.

They both fell into their own bed with nocturnal abandon.
Andrea didn't know what Lily was doing, but from that point
on, all Andrea could do was stare up at the popcorn ceiling. She
was exhausted…but sleep was hiding from her. She wasn't sure
what the happiest topic rushing through her mind was as she
tried to dodge all the anxiety bullets. She had no clear plan for
how to stop Jacob if he decided to fight back *(he could shoot
lightning bolts from his fingertips and cause earthquakes at will)*. She
wasn't entirely sure what the status of her career would be when
she finally reported back to the nearest bureau office *(people had*

been canned for less). And Colin…Colin Fisher *(suspected serial killer, wizard for an evil empire, guy that walked away)* was the most troublesome thought of all.

Why had he left? The analytical profiler side of her brain that she desperately wanted to shut up was generating at least seven different scenarios. The artistic soulful side of her brain was torn between two: either he didn't love her or he loved her too much. Damn it, she wasn't even sure how she felt about him. She couldn't possibly know how he felt about her. They were colleagues. Partners. He had a girlfriend. Who was a suspected assassin. Wanted her dead.

She drifted closer to sleep, occasionally brushing up against it, but never actually crossing into its grip. She looked over at Lily, hoping she was equally insomniac, but was disappointed by her snores. She dutifully flipped through channels, finding nothing particular of interest before giving up and trying fitfully again.

The clock read seventeen past midnight when she pulled out her cell phone and cursed the lack of service. She was desperate, though, and read the number off her phone to dial on the old room telephone. It would be a little after one o'clock Virginia time, right? Late, probably too late. She was about to hang up, when he answered.

"Unghh. Rick Salazar."

She choked a little, suddenly lost as to what to say. "Umm. Good to talk to you, boss."

"Devereaux?" The cobwebs cleared from his voice as he said her name. "What's going on?"

"Long, rough couple of days, boss. I wish I knew where to start."

"Hang on. Let me get this in the study." She could hear some shuffling and thumping in the background as he got out of bed. She nearly fell asleep before his voice returned. "Andrea, you there?"

She nodded, then remember he couldn't see it. "Yeah, boss,

I'm here."

"Got a call today from the acting section chief. Wanted to know if I'd heard from you. Nothing formal, but you're making somebody nervous. Something about a lost rental car and an unauthorized investigation." He paused. "Have I heard from you, Andrea?

"I'll let you figure that out, boss. You always were better at the office politics."

"Fair enough. You all right? Do you need me to round up a posse? I don't start back as section chief again till Monday."

"No, I'm…I'm all right." She stared up at the ceiling. "Just a little heart broken, I think."

There was a long pause on his end. "You and Mr. Fisher?"

"Really!? What, do you have me under surveillance?"

Salazar chuckled. "No, Andrea. I'm a profiler, remember? Supposedly a pretty good one according to what they're offering me to not take early retirement. I had suspected you two since you came to see me in the hospital together."

She was speechless, then said, "Yeah. Me and Colin."

"You going to be okay, dear?"

"I think so, boss. Just kind of confusing right now. I haven't slept in two days, I'm a little nervous about confronting the perp tomorrow…and I really wish he wouldn't have left me this morning."

"Do I need to get my shotgun, go have a talk with that young man about proper manners?" His voice was grim, but still playful.

"No, boss. We never were…We never were anything. I just…I was starting to think we might have been."

"Maybe he did, too. He's a born runner, Andrea. He gets to liking something and there's a part of him that says it's time to run before everything goes to hell in a handbasket."

"I know, boss." She curled up into the pillow with the phone, wishing she was really at his country home in Virginia. "I know I look like her. That's got to be messing with his brain."

"Yes," he said sagely. "But if he really likes you, he'll come back around."

"And what do I do until then, boss?"

"Unofficially? Catch the perp. I've heard rumors about what really happened in Vegas. Whoever did that...get him, Andrea. Even if we can't charge him with it, even if the bosses are determined to sweep it under the rug, get him."

She smiled at that. "Yes, sir...and thank you."

6

COLIN

I set my alarm for six o'clock in the morning. Normally, I wouldn't have considered such an ungodly hour of the day as time to wake up after such a difficult week. But I had a strong suspicion that my door would be rattling under Timmy's potent intrusion soon. I hadn't told anyone I was back in Boston. I was pretty sure Lucien would know anyways. My dreams that night were full of five-headed fang-mouthed sand worms swimming underneath me in burning desert sand. Sometimes a dream is just a dream. I really hoped that was just a dream.

I actually had a little bit of cream and sugar in my morning coffee when the knock came. It wasn't the full-out manic banging of Timmy that I had expected. The knock was a strong, but controlled, tap-tap-tap. I reached out with my senses, feeling for any supernatural aura or danger before I crossed over to open it. Before me, clad in his traditional silver three-piece suit, was Lucien Valente.

He nodded, his well-coiffed black hair obedient and well-managed. "Mr. Fisher."

I tried to keep my shock from showing and nodded back, making sure my jaw didn't hang open. "Mr. Valente?"

"May I enter?"

I stepped back and finished the rest of my coffee with a gulp. "Of course, sir."

He crossed over the threshold and slowly looked around, taking in the massive apartment slash laboratory with a panoramic glance. "I enjoy your sense of style, Mr. Fisher. These relics look far better on display then hidden away in my warehouses."

"Thank you, Mr. Valente." I slowly walked behind him as he paced the perimeter towards the prayer rug wall.

"You made good time from Lafayette to Boston, Mr. Fisher. I was rather surprised to learn you were back home."

"I made a deal with a devil."

He stopped and looked back, with the closest I had ever seen to shock on Valente's disciplined face. "You are full of surprises, Mr. Fisher."

"I try." I paused. "How did you know about Lafayette?"

"Freak sidewalk damage might not have caught my attention, particularly after an unprecedented Colorado earthquake. However, the lamppost wrapped around as if to imprison someone was noteworthy enough that I pulled what footage I could from nearby security cameras."

I thought back, trying to remember any outdoor traffic cameras, but failed. I had a rather disturbing revelation. "Valente International owns a home security company, don't they?"

Lucien grinned at me. "It pays to be well-diversified in today's global economy."

"Is this where you tell me I had no business continuing to chase Darien?"

"No, Mr. Fisher. You seem competent enough against him...and whatever he is doing is weakening. The CRTs, or your FBI friend, will bring him to bay soon enough, I have no doubt. Is she a friend still, Mr. Fisher? Or do I need to give Miss Wakefield specific instructions regarding her continued existence?"

"I'm not sure I understand."

"If you are romantically or sexually involved with her, I can ensure that Miss Wakefield's temper does not get the better of her. Do I need to intervene on her behalf?"

"No," I shook my head. "I don't think so. She's…just a friend."

"I understand the strange tides of the heart, my wizard. In fact, it is to that end that I came to see you. Have you made any progress on the project I asked you about?"

That surprised me, but I tried to not let it show. Romance was not a use for an amnesia potion that I had considered. Truth be told, I had never even considered Lucien Valente and an affair of the heart in the same sentence before, ever. "Six weeks of amnesia in a bottle? I've made a few notes. I'm going to try a couple of preliminary experiments later today."

"I see. And how soon do you expect to have anything ready? I'm afraid I'm on a bit of deadline here."

"A romantic liaison gone wrong? Anything…I should know?"

He stared at the lone eastern window of the massive second floor room. "I have been seeing a young woman for a little over a month now and she is…unreasonably attached to me. I do not mind seeing that she is well provided for, but she has learned things about my business and person that I do not wish to become public knowledge. If I reject her advances, I fear she would spread this information to any tabloid that would listen. I need her to not remember me anymore."

I nodded. "And after you erase her mind?"

"What would you like to hear, Mr. Fisher? I gave you an ethics clause. What treatment of her is fair in this matter? Should she wake up in another city, far from here, with ten grand in her possession? More money? Less? What will make you comfortable in assisting me?"

I thought about it. "What happens to her if I can't come up

with a working elixir or alternative?"

He smirked and a small part of me hated him in that instant. "If I cannot erase her memory...I would be required to erase her."

I sighed, wondering how I was going to live with myself after this. I didn't like the idea of erasing the poor woman's memory, but I didn't cherish the prospect of Veruca murdering her either. "How long do I have?"

"I can give you another three days, Mr. Fisher."

"When you first approached me about it, you said you needed it for them. I expected you to need more than one dose."

His smirk, that despised smirk, stayed firmly in place. "A lot of my relationships go sour, Mr. Fisher."

7

ANDREA

T he new day brought with it new energy. Andrea Devereaux
was cruising south on I-35 just past the Oklahoma border.
By midday, she would be at the Douglas apartment where,
she suspected, Jacob Darien had gone to lick his wounds. From
talking to Lilianna, she was certain her guess was right. He had
been happy there, a private paradise of all the joys he had ever
wanted. It had not been perfect, but it had been what they both
wanted: companionship, shelter, peace, and romance. Lily had
described it yesterday as a crappy ghetto environment with
connections to infinite pocket universes, accessible only to
them.

The scenery wasn't much to see beyond brown, barren,
winter fields. She turned over to Lily, now riding shotgun as
partner, instead of the back seat as suspect. "Tell me more
about the pocket universes."

Lily shook her head, her hair fluttering in front of her face.
"It's hard to explain. Just like nothing else mattered outside of
the two of us. He would tell me stories about books he wanted
to write, or movies he wanted to make, and…it's like the stories
were more real, more solid than our actual lives. I wanted to be
a character in any of them far more than I wanted to be

Lilianna."

Andrea used her years of profiling experience to her advantage and made only a slight encouraging noise to let her know she was listening. This sounded like the sort of story that could only be patiently coaxed out with encouragement, not pried out with interrogation.

A mile passed before Lily continued, "I really was those characters. He would base them off of me and the way he described them, the way he talked about them, made me feel so special, so loved. And I would pick out the characters he was basing on himself...and we'd pretend. I'd be my character and he'd be his and we would bounce dialogue off of each other. I'd react to what was going on in the story like it was me. Sometimes, we'd even take it into the bedroom...." She blushed and stopped.

"He really loves you, doesn't he?"

She nodded, tears starting to roll down her cheeks. "Yeah. Yeah, he does. I think this is why this hurts so much." She sniffled through the oncoming cry. "I keep telling myself that this is helping him, that he needs to be protected from...whatever is going wrong with him and David and Reverend...but all at the same time, it feels like I'm betraying that love."

Andrea tried to find the right psychology response, as if she were interviewing a witness, and found she could only speak as a friend. "I wish I could tell you what's ahead for the two of you. I suspect he's going to have some years in prison, if he ever really wants to get past this. But... there's no reason the two of you can't go on. Even prisons have visiting days. And he'll be free someday. Right now, just focus on figuring out who you want to be, how you can support yourself...and then be there for him when you can be."

Her attempts at comfort appeared lost on the building tear storm. "I just want to disappear into a hoodie and not come out, ever." In between tears, Lily asked, "Do you really think he loves me?"

Andrea took a deep gulp and gripped the steering wheel tighter. "I'm betting my life on it."

8

COLIN

I couldn't stop thinking about Andrea as I worked that day. I told myself it was strictly out of concern for her well-being. If Jacob was where she thought he was, she would be face-to-face with a renegade wizard of phenomenal power any time now. I had nearly gone down to Timmy's apartment twice to ask to borrow his phone. I had serious doubts as to whether my concern was merely for her safety or not.

I really needed to sort out that whole train of thought before anything went too much further. Soon, Veruca would be back from her assignment in Chicago, and I wanted to know what I was supposed to tell her and how everything fit into my future plans regarding the pharmaceutical drugs that Valente had assured me would be there later that afternoon. I wanted to think my plans regarding those were flexible, a cup that could be taken from me, but the truth was my feet were set on that path from the moment I dreamed of Sarai from deep inside a coma. What the hell was I supposed to say to Veruca? Or Devereaux for that matter?

The second rule of wizarding, if there is such an official thing, is focus. When tackling a project, I needed to really, truly have my attention on it. Otherwise, I ended up with exploding telephones thwacking me upside the head. As much as I wanted to resolve those nagging questions, if I was going to beat Lucien's deadline, I needed my attention firmly on amnesia potions. Did it bother me that they were intended to erase knowledge of sex and romance? Maybe, but given how much I wished I could forget my last six weeks of heart stuff, there were a lot worse things Lucien could be asking me to design.

I had sent out word for reinforcements when the birds were most active, around seven in the morning. It was the kind of call that few knew how to make. I knew both enough to make it and enough to be nervous about the consequences. I had spelled out Selena's name in birdseed on my western windowsill, where the night's shadow still lingered, then infused it with a bit of my will. It was not the surest way to call her, but it was polite and subtle. I wanted Kerath's fiancée here because she wanted to be here, not because I was strong enough and dumb enough to trap her in a magical circle.

"What happened to do not meddle in the affairs of the fae, for you are crunchy and will taste good with catsup…after they turn you into a frog?"

"I still think you're butchering that quote. But I agree with the intent."

"Scary when we agree about something."

"Even more so when we agree and yet we do the opposite anyway."

"Yep. So…what's up with the drugs?"

"Maybe they'll help if we can't figure out a strictly herbal concoction."

I turned my attention towards my herb cabinets, taking an inventory of what I had in stock, and hoping Yog didn't go too deep in to my brain meats about the pharmacy package. Every wizard kept secrets; I just had to keep mine from myself, too. There were plenty of herbs with modern associations towards helping people remember…but forgetting required older knowledge. No one wanted a pill to help them forget. I mentally tried to recall what the pages had looked like in the nineteenth century French alchemy text, but found my focus wasn't what it once had been. I wished I still had the book, but it was one I had read back when my library size was dictated by the space available in the trunk of my car.

"You called, Wizard Fisher?" Her voice was soft and lyrical, but even at the distance from my dining table to my kitchen, I heard her as clearly as if she were in my ear.

I turned to greet her, offering a deep bow, before responding. "I did invite, Lady Selena. I am glad you accepted it, though I expected you by the door."

Much as I had seen her before, Selena was too thin, impossibly angular in the face, but still radiantly beautiful. She was a creature of a different land, a vision most men would have carved their eyes out to see only once. She sat leisurely reclined in one of the dark green chairs with purple blooms that she and Kerath had given me last Thanksgiving in gratitude for saving his life. Kerath was a troll. Selena was…I wasn't entirely sure. She was of the Unseelie court and blood, but most people who dabbled in fae hierarchy were criminally insane, even before they started writing their opuses on the fairies.

She smiled up at me from the recesses of the dusky chair. "Is this business or pleasure, Wizard Fisher? Should I be charging Valente International for my time?"

I forced my best cocky wizard grin on my face. "I am in Valente's employ, personal wizard on his behalf, and on an assignment for his interests." I relaxed the facial mask. "But I am in the company of friends, right?"

"Careful, wizard. My beloved has told me all about your negotiation skills." She fixed her icy blue eyes on me and it sent shivers down my spine. "But I am not opposed to casual discussion with you. What can I do for you?"

This was where I needed to be most careful. If she saw her service as a favor to me, and one that I was not currently suited to repay, I would owe her. And owing the fae is kind of like owing a loan shark, except the loan shark can only break your physical legs. "I am researching an elixir to help mortal minds forget the last six weeks of their existence. It is a tight deadline and I'm running out of ideas."

"Hmm." Her grin was intoxicating. "There are numerous blossoms in the dark depths of the Faewild that could accomplish that and more with but a single sip of their nectar. But even for one of your skill and stature, retrieving the blooms would not be easy. I think that may, perhaps, do more damage than what you are intending."

"Six weeks," I said, firmly. "I don't want to take more than I absolutely have to. And something that can be recreated in the physical world is preferable."

"Those flowers I mentioned have reflections in your world, for once the two worlds were one. I believe you call them belladonna lilies."

I nodded sagely. "They do have associations with helping someone forget past loves. But their potency is not to the degree of their fae world counterparts."

"If I were a wizard," she said, with careful lyrical precision, "I would look to split the difference between the two. Weakening the potency of the fae bloom might be possible, but it is inaccessible. But harvest the physical blossom under the right correspondences and strengthen its action with enchantment and you may be able to achieve your desired effect. I would take it at night, at the darkest part of the night, and pluck it by hand, not by blade. That should get you the raw ingredients. The enchantment, I trust, is more your field of expertise?"

"My dear Selena, from the stories I have heard, I would not want to stand against you in a contest of sorcery."

"You flatter me, dear wizard. And since all I gave you was words, should we call it a fair trade at that? My words of wisdom for your words of praise?" She paused and I suddenly felt more at risk. "Or would you like to trade with me for a sample of the dark blooms that grow in the deepest reaches of the Faewild? I think you might have much to offer that would entice me, Wizard Fisher."

I shook my head, trying to forcibly clear the entanglements

of her voice from my mind. "Praise will suffice for now. Should I offer more to make it fair? You are wise and just, Lady Selena, a rare bloom from the darkness yourself."

"So cautious, wizard. You might do well to indebt yourself to a member of the court. You avoid it so prodigiously it is becoming something of a prize among those who care about such things. Should you ever wish a mistress less harsh than might otherwise trap you, you have only to ask. But I will not take you by force." She stood from the embrace of the petaled chair. "Is our business done for the day? Or would you like to consider another matter?"

"I fear business is done, Lady Selena. But my hospitality is available. Would you like something to eat and drink?"

She laughed. "I remember your Thanksgiving Dinner all too well. I do not mean to be rude, but I think I do not have time to wait for the pizza man today."

I laughed, too. "Fair enough, Selena. Thank you for coming."

"Thank you for having me, Wizard Fisher."

9

VERUCA

They stood in the second subbasement of Valente International's corporate headquarters, but for all intents and purposes, they may as well have been back in a casino basement in Vegas. Veruca scratched that thought and rewrote it to include that Valente International was better equipped for such situations than mobsters ever could have been. This particular level, and the three underneath it, had been designed to withstand full-scale tactical assault by professional military forces. The entrance was not obvious to those who did not know of the existence of this section of Valente International. The soundproofing between this floor and the legitimate basement above made it certain that no one could have heard the man's screams, even if he had still been awake to scream.

There had been no hesitation in this interrogation. Maybe it was because he was a man or maybe because he appeared to have chosen his affiliation, rather than to have been brainwashed into it. Or maybe, with a few days away from Colin, Veruca was losing her human edge, regressing to the demon-blooded assassin the world had groomed her to be. Her handwashing this time was entirely mechanical, not a ritual guilt cleansing.

"Do you believe him, Deluce?"

She shook her head, her gaze still fixed on the interrogation cell where the medical staff was tending to their guest. "Not entirely, Miss Wakefield. He has been well trained to resist torture and mental magic. The combination approach, over time, should peel back the layers to uncover his deepest secrets."

"Yeah." Veruca scrubbed the last of the soap off her hands. "I think he's still holding out on us, too. Still…gave us a few things to work with. Any results from the lab?"

Duchess broke telepathic contact with their victim to consult a small silver tablet. "85% pure heroin. That's strange. The lab is having trouble conclusively identifying the other 15%. High-grade product. If I had to guess, the unidentified part may require the use of Valente's wizard. The Faceless seem to have a penchant for the mystical."

"No," Veruca said firmly. "Colin stays out of this. It's bad enough that there's a worldwide secret organization devoted to hunting down and killing wizards. The last thing I need is for my favorite wizard to start looking for them. We handle this."

"Istanbul? You may need to call in some outside help, Miss Wakefield. Last I heard, Lucien had revoked your ability to enter the countries of Turkey, Syria, and Lebanon."

"A girl starts one little riot and now I've got a no-fly zone. Really, Duchess, I was hardly involved."

"Forgetting that I am in your mind, Miss Wakefield?"

She dried her hands on a clean towel. "No…just hoping you wouldn't feel the need to be a total bitch for once."

"Ouch. That hurt, Miss Wakefield. Here I was thinking about suitable arrangements to find you a partner for this mission."

Veruca drilled holes into Miss Deluce with her eyes and wished she could make them literal holes. "What are you up to?"

"Mmm." She smiled. "I'll let you know after Mr. Valente signs off on it."

10

ANDREA

L ily and Devereaux both sat in the car, pulled over to the side of the street, staring at the gap in the white walls that signaled the entrance to the apartment complex. All around them, a bright sunny day held court. But above the complex, localized only to the skies above the apartments, black storm clouds rumbled and churned ominously. If Andrea had any doubt about where Jacob Darien was, it had been erased. But knowing where the monster was and having the courage to enter its den were proving to be two different things. They both sat, staring, wondering what new terror this way came.

Andrea's phone rang from her jacket, startling them both. B-na-nana-nana-na! B-na-nana-nana-na! She dug for it, suddenly afraid the wizard she hunted could hear its chime. "Agent Devereaux speaking."

Colin's voice staticked on the other end. "Yeah, umm, hey."

"Hey, yourself. Where are you?" There were a million questions fighting to be spoken, but that was the first out her lips.

"Back in Boston. Long story. You?"

She fought not to say that she was wishing he was here. "Looking at Jacob's apartment complex. He's here all right."

"You've got this. I know you do." His voice disappeared for a moment into the background of a parking lot pay phone. "If I thought you couldn't handle it, I'd be there."

"Mr. Fisher, is that concern I hear in your voice? I don't usually expect that from partners who abandon me mid-investigation."

"Yeah. Well, it's complicated."

Before her brain-to-mouth editor could intervene, it slipped out. "Because I look like her?"

The lack of immediate reply on the other end answered the question. "That's...that's part of it. The fact that my live-in girlfriend kills people for a living is another. I prefer you alive."

"I prefer you alive, too. Friends? Can we still be friends, Colin?"

There was a pause before his voice returned a tad more playful. "Hey, I'm calling to make sure Darien didn't eat you, aren't I? Of course, we can be friends. And...I just need some more time. Need to get some answers about what really happened to Sarai. Then, maybe...."

"Yeah. I get it. Let's not make this any weirder than it has to be. I've got a weather-manipulating rogue wizard to bring in."

"And I've got a few memories to erase. Sounds like a busy day all around." His voice came back somber. "Be careful, Andrea. And... can you call me after you're done? I'd like to know you're okay."

"Call you? I didn't realize you even had a phone number."

"Oh. Well, I don't, but I've got a messaging service thingy...umm, Timmy, I've got a Timmy. Let me give you his number."

Andrea took it down, then said goodbye to him. The hardest part was resisting the urge to say, "I love you," as she hung up the phone.

11

COLIN

I stared at the parking lot payphone for far longer than I probably should have, given the number of times my life had been in danger in recent months. I had friend-zoned her, right? That was what people called it nowadays. She didn't feel very friend zone at all. I wanted to stand there, staring, waiting for Timmy to come and tell me that she was okay, that Jacob was dead, and that she wanted to marry me. Okay, maybe, I didn't want to hear all those things in that specific order, but I did want to know she was all right.

"You can still save her, if you want. I could have us there in under a minute."

"If we go, either Jacob dies or we die."

"I'd rip him apart before he even realized we were inside his apartment."

"You'd like that, wouldn't you? A little wholesale carnage and chaos, a chance to wreck a building?"

"You know me so well, Colin."

"Yeah, I do. And we're not going. If he hurts her, if something happens to Andrea... I'll let you take revenge. But we're going to do our best to resolve this the right way."

"Sometimes the right way involves tentacles and terror. If we'd taken

that approach with the wendigo, your left ear wouldn't be such a mess."

"Shut up."

"Really? Back to this? How childish."

"You and I aren't forever, Yog. One of these days I'm going to find out what you did with Sarai...and then I'm sending you back beyond the outer walls of space and time."

"Good luck with that. I ate her. With a nice chianti."

"Again, shut up...wait a second."

"What?"

"You don't know."

"Don't know what? I'm an elder god, a terror beyond the comprehension of mortals. What don't I know?"

"You don't know what happened to her, do you? You're just as clueless as I am."

"What makes you think that? I ate her. Every last bite."

"No. If you knew, you'd show me. You'd slam my mind with the image of her last moments, the vision of her flesh sliding down my throat. But you can't...because you don't remember what happened that night any more than I do."

Silence followed, then... *"Sometimes you're smarter than you look, Fisher. It's what makes us such a scary-good team."*

I did my best to ignore his flattery, satisfied that I had learned something at last about Sarai. I had also learned a thing or two from my time with Veruca and for once noticed my surroundings: Veruca's latest motorcycle cruised into the parking lot, distracting me from both my internal conversation and my external worries. For better or for worse, Andrea Deverereaux was on her own against the most powerful wizard I had ever witnessed.

I jogged back towards Veruca and the apartment, wondering what the hell I was going to say to her.

12

ANDREA

The door to 702 was partially ajar, a meager black crack at the edge of the gray door. The air outside was cold and thick, fitting to the bleakest of February days, but vibrating as if rattled by a source of immense energy. Andrea knocked on the door, her gun out and flat against her leg in her other hand. "FBI! We're coming in!"

No response came as she flung open the door and surveyed the living room. She double checked the recliners in the corner, half expecting to see a strange black man in one of them. There was none. Andrea was alone. She carefully checked the kitchen, making sure to let nothing between her and the open door she had come through. "Jacob! I know you're in here. I just want to talk. Can we talk, Jacob?"

There was nothing but darkness and silence for a moment. Then his voice came, weak, different than before, from the master bedroom. "Go away, FBI."

Andrea crept to the edge of the bedroom door. "It doesn't work like that, Jacob. Even for guys like you, there are rules. One of them is you need to talk to me if you want to fix any of this."

"Fix it?" He laughed, a sad, dark sound. "I'll fix it in a

moment."

She summoned all her courage and kicked down the door. Her gun came up to fire. Her eyes scanned the room as she entered. The suspect was on the back corner of the queen-size bed, facing her. He held a small gun, a .38 special, in one hand. Had it been pointed at her, she would have pulled her trigger. But Jacob had his barrel firmly pressed against his own head. She trained her gun on him, uncertain of what to do. She focused, lowered her weapon. "Jacob, don't do this."

"You wanted it fixed?" He clicked back the hammer of the gun. "This should do the trick. The money...what's left of it...is under the bed. The rest got lost mid-teleport. Now, leave. Unless you want to watch."

She took a deep breath. "Those the bullets you made yourself?"

His hazel eyes locked onto her. "Yeah. How did you know?"

"Depleted uranium rounds. Hard to acquire everything you'd need. Why? You never pulled the trigger during a robbery."

He shook his head, the gun slipping and swaying on his skin as he did. "Bullets ain't for people."

"Monsters? Spirit things?"

"Yeah. Uranium is so real, so heavy. Good stopping power, but it's real...even when other things aren't."

She nodded, wishing she knew where she was going with this. "Why did you make those, Jacob? You didn't need them to rob people."

"No, no." He shook his head and for a second, Andrea thought his gun would go off. "They were for...saving people. Helping people against things they can't see."

"Like the monsters in your nightmares? Fighting off those?"

He frowned. "I don't want to talk about it. Just...just leave. I've screwed up everything."

"Let me offer you a small fix, Jacob. Can I offer you a small fix? My name is Andrea or Agent Devereaux. Use whichever you like."

"What...what can you possibly offer me? What deal could I believe?"

"I get that. Someone is going to want to prosecute you for the armed robberies you were a part of. I can't say what they'll want or why. But that's the way the system works. People get arrested, Jacob. They get a record and then they're at the mercy of the courts. I want to arrest you, Jacob. But if you'll put that gun down, give me the gun, I won't arrest Lily. I ignore the gun charge, the assault on a federal officer. You give me the gun; Lily goes free."

He laughed, a little less macabre than the first. "Hell of an offer. Always wanted to spend the rest of my life in a tiny cell."

"Yeah, but you're thinking about it all the same, Jacob. I can't save you from the system. But I can save Lily. And maybe...just maybe...you do your time, get out someday, and you and she...." Andrea let it trail intentionally.

Jacob's hand followed her train of thought, the gun slowly dropping from his head. "They're gone, you know. Reverend, David... They're gone. It's just me in here now. Lily... Lily wouldn't want me anyway."

Andrea holstered her gun and moved closer to the bed. "You might be surprised, Jacob. I've spent the last couple of days with her." She slid onto the bed, her right hand outstretched for his gun. "I don't agree with what you did. But I don't know that I've ever seen two people who loved each other more."

He put the gun into her palm. "You know I could still take you, right? One blast of magic and...."

She nodded, watching as he cried. "I know, Jacob. I know you could. I'm glad you're not."

He let go. "Maybe it's time I stopped. No more magic for a while."

She tucked his gun away and dared to wrap her arms around

him. "It'll be okay, Jacob. No more magic for a while. I'll help you out, anyway I can. Just...let's get the healing started. I'll take you to turn yourself in for the robberies. You play ball with the courts, no lightning bolts to the judge. I'll pull some strings to get you the easiest appropriate sentence that I can. I'll even look in on Lily from time to time when I can, make sure she's okay."

Jacob Darien, apprehended fugitive and notorious terrorist, sobbed into her shoulder for longer than either of them would ever admit to another living being.

13

COLIN

"How was Chicago?" I hoped my tone was light enough, appropriate enough, to disguise my inner turmoil.

"Fine," she said, nonchalantly. Maybe a little too nonchalantly.

"Take in a Cubs game? Or is Valente part of the infamous curse?"

She laughed. "First, you hate baseball. Second, it's February, which you might know if you didn't hate baseball. Third, maybe he is. I know he goes to watch the Red Sox at least twice a year." She paused at the entry way to our kitchen. "So, what's up? You never ask about my work. And…do I really want to know why a mad science experiment has overgrown the kitchen?"

"Oh, yeah, that," I said, trying to stretch out the work conversation. "A project for Valente. Distillation of belladonna essence into a tincture, on a time crunch. Normally, you let it soak in the alcohol for a week, but I'm on a schedule."

She eyeballed it all cautiously. "Isn't belladonna toxic or something? Is it safe to have in our kitchen?"

"Given our cooking skills, I've been relying on takeout pretty heavily anyway. There's a new Mongolian BBQ place a

couple of blocks over. It's way safer than our kitchen." I
stepped up behind her, my body close to hers. "Care to make it
a date?"

She turned, looked up at me, and put her arms around my
neck. If this was combat maneuvering, it was a technique I
hadn't seen before. She stared into my eyes. "Sure you didn't fall
for the beautiful FBI agent bodyguard?"

I nodded. "She's all right. A good friend. But…" I switched
effortlessly from English to Russian. "…she lacks a certain
element of dangerous beauty."

"Mmm, I do like that barbaric tongue…and no beauty is
more dangerous than me. Except maybe Duchess. Damn
telepath."

I smiled. "So are we going to talk about other women or go
eat Mongolian BBQ until we're stuffed and can't move?"

She purred back in French. "I didn't hear anything about me
molesting you in either of those options."

I pulled back a little, not a conscious decision, but we both
noticed it. "Veruca…I'm not sure that's a great idea."

"That would be why they call it molestation. But why?
What's wrong?"

"I…I've got a couple of projects I need to take care of…
and I'm worried about a lot of things."

"Colin…don't do this to me." Her voice was soft, distant.

I shouldn't have said anything, shouldn't have started down
this conversational path. But I did. So what the hell was I
supposed to say now? "Veruca, I'm not…I'm not doing
anything to you. Just not sure I'm the best person in the world
for anyone to be attached to right now."

"The assassins? Suddenly worried I can't take care of
myself? Don't worry, Colin. I'm going to wipe every last one of
them off the planet." Her voice grew proud and ominous. "I've
already started with a few dozen of them."

Yog's reaction inside of me and my own could not have
been any more different. He was ready to party in celebration. I

just felt nauseous. "No. I mean, maybe they're right. Yog Soggoth is dangerous. Maybe he needs killing."

"Colin…no one, and I mean no one, is going to hurt you if I can help it. I don't care how dangerous Yog-whatever is. You're not. You're safe and kind and wonderful…and the world is a better place for having you in it."

I kissed her softly, then desperation took over and we both kissed back deeply. When we parted, I confessed, "I'm not excited about dying myself. But if I don't want them to do it… maybe I need to take care of the problem myself."

Her eyes dug into mine, searching for my secrets. "What are you planning, my little wizard?"

I shook my head. "Can we…can we just have a nice date? Eat some Chinese food, people-watch, talk about nothing at all. Pretend like we're normal?"

She kissed my cheek. "Of course, my love. Of course." She squeezed me tightly.

I almost told her everything. But that would have ruined it, because Yog would have heard my plan too. I would just have to hope that Veruca would forgive me later. I might have spilled the beans, but an overly-excited pounding on my apartment door saved me from my own mouth.

14

ANDREA

A ndrea left a message with Timmy. She wasn't sure what she had expected from anyone Valente used to pass messages, but it certainly wasn't that. She was pretty sure that voice belonged to a caricature of an overly-excited self-esteem counselor for elementary school children. She didn't wait for him to get Colin, even though he offered...repeatedly. She could only deal with one emotionally laden wizard at a time, but she did want him to know both Jacob and she were okay.

Lily stayed in the passenger seat, even when Andrea put a handcuffed Jacob into the back seat. She was turned around, her head beside the headrest, looking back at him. They didn't talk, didn't touch...but Agent Devereaux didn't think they needed to. Their silent looks conveyed more information than most people's long conversations. She tried to follow their lack of discussion as best she could, but she needed to drive and still wasn't overly familiar with Oklahoma City. She knew she had been to the county jail here before on a previous assignment, but found that she really couldn't remember the experience, as if it was drowned in a watery fog.

She had no idea what to do with Jacob. Technically, the FBI had dropped the investigation into the robberies in Arizona and the battle in Vegas. If she turned him into the nearest federal office, he would undoubtedly be diverted to whatever secret military outfit that was interested in either neutralizing or weaponizing Jacob's talents. But she had no authority, on her own, to do anything else.

Andrea pulled over into an empty parking lot and retrieved her phone. She quickly googled the Midwest City Police, scanned through their information, and dialed a number.

"Midwest City Police Department, Detective Carr speaking."

Andrea switched to her best official voice. "This is Special Agent Andrea Devereaux. How are you doing today?"

That seemed to wake up the sleepy drawl on the other end. "I'm okay. I didn't realize we had any joint operations right now."

"We don't. I was looking into something else and came across something of interest to your department, I think. I have a suspect willing to confess to a local liquor store robbery. He doesn't want to go into federal custody, though, and I'd prefer to keep my name out of it. You know any detectives who might like that collar?"

Andrea could hear his gears grinding through the phone. After a long thoughtful pause, Detective Carr's voice returned. "Liquor store robbery on Douglas? Yeah, I remember the one. Weird case. Why doesn't he want to do his time in Club Fed?"

"Can I trust you, Detective Carr?"

He chuckled a little. "If you call me Daniel, then yes, yes you can."

"Daniel, between you and me, if the wrong feds get hold of him I think he disappears into some Guantanamo-like black hole never to be heard from again. He's got…some special skills."

"So an on-record arrest publicly, in a state that's not known for being willing to share its prisoners with the feds, is the best chance he's got of doing time and going home?" Pause. "What kind of special skills? Never mind; I saw the security system stuff at the liquor store. Must be a heckuva tech guy."

"You could say that. Can I trust you, Daniel? You want to call a press conference and show yourself taking him into custody?"

"I'd want to interview him first. Make sure I understand the facts of the case well enough to not sound like an idiot. You want to bring him by the station? Or do I need to meet you someplace else?"

Andrea looked at the two lovebirds, still pining from each other at a distance, tears rolling down both faces. "Either of you want a last lunch?"

Neither of them replied, still lost in whatever secret they were sharing.

Andrea turned back to the phone. "I seem to remember a decent onion burger last time I was in town. You got a favorite place that can do that?"

His chuckle was a comforting break to the somberness around her. "You know, now that you mention it, it is getting awfully close to my lunch break. You want to meet me at Ron's Hamburgers?"

"Yeah. I think that will work, Daniel. And thanks."

15

COLIN

Veruca and I were always at our best when we pretended we were just normal folk. Skipping on the way to the restaurant, making fishie lips at the aquarium in the foyer, stuffing ourselves silly, laughing, laughing, laughing. It was easy with her in times like that to forget who and what we both were, to forget that, for so many people, we were the stuff of nightmares. Once upon a time, I might have thought the demon-blooded assassin at the table was the horror. But the longer we were together, the more I learned about Yog Soggoth, the more certain I was about who the real terror at the table was. The Walker in Shadows was slowly poisoning the sanity of the world through the connection that I gave him to it.

"You say that like it's a bad thing. Human sanity is highly overrated."

I ignored him and tried to focus on finishing the project for Lucien. The date had been fun, hearing that Jacob had surrendered to Andrea was great, but I had work to finish.

"And then you can turn your attention to the side project that you don't want me to know about?"

"And you still don't know about it."

"You contemplating suicide, Colin? Off both of us in one smooth stroke?"

"It wouldn't work and we both know it. I'd die and you would enslave someone else... eventually. And Sarai, wherever she is, would stay stuck forever."

"All very true. Doesn't mean you're not dumb enough to try."

"Nope. I've got something else in mind for you."

"The extra potion you're brewing? Don't think I didn't notice that you're making six copies for Lucien and a seventh on a slightly different recipe."

I cursed his observant eyes and returned to my alchemy. Selena had been kind enough to point me in the right direction. Now it was just a matter of balancing out the elixir before infusing the magic. The seventh was indeed related to Yog Soggoth, but more as a red herring than a silver bullet. So long as he was eyeballing the vial as the real danger to him, I thought I had a chance to pull this off.

The recipe was simple enough: an accelerated tincture of belladonna and vodka, mixed with a few drops of dragon's blood and a tincture of lotus leaf that I already had lying around to give it a magical kick. Six counter-clockwise stirs in each bottle, followed by the incantation. Even if the spell failed, the alcohol alone was enough to leave its recipient dazed and confused for a night. The herbal additions would add in memory loss and religious hallucinations. But to really get the specific kick that Lucien Valente wanted, I needed to bring the magic.

"Six by six, vials and stirs,

"Time unwinds, its memory replaced.

"Six by six, stirs and weeks,

"Mind erodes, life's course forgot.

"Six by six, lines and verses,

"Hear my cry, remove the past."

Over each individual bottle I chanted that six times, gathering my energy, then sealing it in with a plain wooden cork. The elixir would work; I had faith in that. The seventh I sealed without any incantation, then placed it in the center of my embedded silver ritual circle in the center of my apartment workspace.

"*No last words, no spell to help its chances?*"

"*I'll wait so that the magic is still fresh when I use it.*"

"*Curiouser and curiouser.*"

Yog Soggoth's many eyes were firmly on that bottle as I wrote out a note to Lucien to put with the elixirs I had made:

Dear sir,

These bottles should accomplish the effect you wanted me to create. I apologize that I am unable to deliver them in person, as I am in the middle of a magical working of a personal nature. I trust that these will find their way to you and you will consider my duties as personal wizard fulfilled until I am finished with my own project. Thank you for your patronage.

Respectfully,
Colin Fisher

I disrobed and crept around to the bed where Veruca still slept, either exhausted from our date or from the large quantity of alcohol that I encouraged her to drink. I kissed her softly on the forehead, then retrieved the black silk robe I had acquired for ritual work. There really were advantages to being a well-funded wizard. I added my chaos blade to the right pocket and checked to make sure the contents of the left pocket were still there. With everything present, I entered the circle, ready to begin the ritual.

With the chaos blade, I sealed the circle, walking clockwise along its length, the blade tip hovering just above the metal ring. That done, I knelt in front of the seventh vial of belladonna tincture.

"*No chanting, no chalk outlines. What are you up to, Colin?*"

"*I'm going to go talk to Sarai again. Find out more about my past lives, who I really am.*"

"*More? I'm missing something. That cocktail is just going to help you forget."*

"You are absolutely right. That's why I'm not going to drink it."

"But then, how...?"

I pulled the needle out of my left pocket, jabbing it into my thigh as hard as I could, pushing desperately at the plunger before Yog could take control.

"Ouch. Tricky boy, Colin. Dirty pool."

"Midazolam. Intermuscular injection with an insanely high dose for my height and weight."

"I'm not up on modern pharmacology, Colin. What exactly are you expecting it to do, turn back time? Take everything back to before we ate her?"

"Nope. Doesn't need to. I know where she is now. Just need to wait. Five minutes? Maybe less."

"And then... death. No, coma? You saw her while you were out in Vegas!"

I could feel his rage building, even as the medication started to spread. Yog Soggoth wrestled his way to the controls of my brain, tentacles sprouting from my pores.

*"Self-induced coma? Are you insane? Do you have any idea the chances you have of waking up...**ever**???"*

Yog battled and thrashed, trying to move out past the circle and failing. He threw himself, extraplanar dimensions and all, at Veruca, hoping to wake her. But the circle held.

"Not to seal magic in or keep enemies out...to keep me in. Colin...you dirty...dirty...I'll make you pay for this."

"Maybe. But that would mean I have to live through this. Relax, you Cthulhu wannabe, we'll just drift off...and I'll come back when I'm darn ready to. Or I'll die and that will...that will...that will solve another set of problems. No more Walker in Shadows."

"Bastard. This isn't over."

"It is...it is for now."

EPILOGUE

M alachi carefully sliced open the envelope so recently delivered to him with a single swipe of his fingernail. He was back in more comfortable territory now, safely manipulating events from his carnival home on the outskirts of Atlanta. Bob's Funland might have looked like a slightly rundown B-level theme park to mortal eyes…but even Lilith, Queen of Hell, would hesitate to challenge Malachi here in his home sanctuary.

How many homes had he held since he chose eternal death over the vagaries of life? He could count them back to the Moorish invasion of Spain, but beyond that Malachi had lost track. He had known Lilith longer still, when the elegant spires of Atlantis stood tall and proud, radiant in the sunlight that Malachi had not seen since. The game still continued, but the moves grew deep and desperate. The endgame was coming and all the ancients knew it.

He unfolded the letter, carefully. It had been written on torn sheets of yellow legal pad with tight pencil marks. Even touching the letter, Malachi could see Jacob writing it in his mind's eye: Golf pencil in hand, his mattress on the floor of a one-man cell that had been refitted to hold three, his heart intent on his craft.

My dearest Lily,

I'm sorry. That's probably going to be the start of most of my letters for a while. I'm really sorry. At least you know, beyond a shadow of a doubt, that at least one person really meant it when they said they would do anything for you. I started a lot of trouble for you... but I hope I get some credit for turning myself in for you, too. Goddess, I really am sorry.

It's quiet in here. I'm sleeping well. Clean conscience makes for a good night's sleep. I confessed to everything with Detective Carr. He knows things I've done wrong that he probably never even wanted to know about. Not sure how many states and/or governments are going to be trying to charge me with something. So far it's just Oklahoma. I... I don't know how to write this next part, because I'm scared you won't want me anymore, but... it's just me in here now. David is gone. Reverend, too. Just little old Jacob Darien now.

I...I've struggled with suicide. A lot. I want to believe that, if I kill myself, if I just end it, that I'll drift off to the Summerlands and be able to wait for you there. I'd like that. I don't want to go through what I know I'm going to have to go through. Years and years without you in dark places, doing things I'm not proud of to survive. But maybe...maybe I need to live, to break the cycle, to get free of the darkness that's haunted both of us our whole lives.

They had me on suicide watch at first. Can't blame them. I tried after I gave my full confession. Even asked to borrow Carr's gun, save the courts time and money. So they stuffed me in a cell with a hospital gown, a bed, and a toilet...nothing else. Somebody had decorated in there at some point. There was Jesus crap all over every wall: Crosses, Bible verses, Jesus name written in gangland style lettering. Pissed me off. Only in Oklahoma, right?

But I don't know. Something strange happened after my third day in there. I...I prayed. And it felt right. I asked for a sign: told God I'd believe in Him if He could just get me off suicide watch and into general population that same day. Turns out that it was President's Day and I had zero chance of seeing the psychiatrist and getting him to approve my move. So God, big surprise, doesn't exist… Except the psychiatrist did come in on the state holiday and did make his rounds that night. Put me on lithium bicarbonate and decided I was stable enough to move to genpop.

So…I'm reading the Bible. Trying this whole Christian thing. I'm older now. Surely the priests won't be interested in me at this age, right? I don't know. If God wants me to live badly enough to send in a psychiatrist on a holiday, I guess I can stick around a bit longer. It also gives me a reason why I don't just walk out the door. I want to. Goddess, I want to. There are moments that all I can think about is the force wave spell that will rip the cell door off its track and toss it across the cell block. But…I need to pay for what I've done. Maybe it won't be as bad as we think. First offense (that I've ever been caught on), maybe it will only be 5, 10 years?

I hope so. Will you…will you wait for me? Are you even still interested in me now that there's just one of me and not three? I look forward to your next letter regardless of the answer. I've included a visiting form, in case you can get your grandma to bring you. I miss you so much. So so much.

I'm sorry, Lily. I would rather be homeless with you than in the presidential suite without you. I love you.

Yours forever,
Jacob Darien

Malachi carefully folded up the letter, slid it back into its envelope, and stashed it in between books on his bookcase. There was a marginal portion of him that still had enough of a heart to feel for the pain he was going to induce in two young people by making sure that letter never reached its intended destination. It was that nostalgia that induced the elder vampire to keep the letter rather than destroy it outright. But he needed to create distance between the mated pair. There were simply too many temptations for him to resort to magic, if he remained attached to the girl. He needed Jacob Darien desperate, discordant, for the next stages of his plan to work.

That attended to, he reached out with his mind, stretching beyond himself to check on the other two. Stephen Green was in New Orleans still, under the watchful eye of Eliza. That was well enough. Soon, he would be moving into position for his showdown with the fallen death angel. The lord knight...the lord knight remained beyond Malachi's vision, sealed away in a magic circle. Malachi could sense the conflict past the barrier: eldritch aberration versus last lord knight of Atlantis. Only one of them would remain when the circle came down. Malachi would have given anything to know which one of them would win. Perhaps more than the machinations of any of the other players, that battle would decide how the game would finally end.

THE END

Thank you for reading! Find book three of the Modern Knights novels coming soon.

Please sign up for the City Owl Press newsletter for chances to win special subscriber-only contests and giveaways as well as receiving information on upcoming releases and special excerpts.

Joshua Bader

www.facebook.com/joshua.bader.50

All reviews are welcome and appreciated. Please consider leaving one on your favorite social media and book buying sites.

For books in the world of romance and speculative fiction that embody Innovation, Creativity, and Affordability, check out City Owl Press at www.cityowlpress.com.

ACKNOWLEDGEMENTS

The following acknowledgments will most certainly miss multiple people of great importance… You have my sincerest apologies for the oversight and my deepest gratitude for your contributions.

I want to thank my wife and children for the patience and tolerating those times when I disappear into the zone of my own little fictional world. They are both my reason for publishing and my surest ground when I need to return to reality.

I want to thank both Yelena Casale and Tina Moss for their help in editing the book and their belief in my voice. I still believe this is the beginning of great things for all of us at City Owl Press. I would be remiss not include all the City Owl Press authors and the group Facebook discussion for their encouragement and inspiration, most notably Danielle DeVor and EJ Wenstrom.

I certainly did not invent the genre of urban fantasy. While I first met it in the works of C.S. Lewis, I owe a deep debt to Stephen King, Dean Koontz, Jim Butcher, and Laurell Hamilton for developing both the genre and my imagination. Of my characters are half as real to the reader as Harry Dresden or Anita Blake are to me, then I am honored.

I owe a debt to those groups of gamers who let me practice and develop my storytelling voice and the individual names would overwhelm the size of this page. Whether it was in my home, yours, or at one or our live actions settings, I thank you for the opportunity and hope you all had as much fun as I did. Tim and Joe, I owe special thanks to both of you..

ABOUT THE AUTHOR

Joshua Bader is a retired professional vagabond wizard who now leads a much more settled life in Oklahoma City. He dabbles in the mystic arts of writing, mathematics education, pizza delivery, and parenting. He shares his sacred space with his wife, two daughters, three dogs, and a cat, with a baby boy adding to the chaos in April 2016. Josh holds a masters in psychology from OU, but his wizarding license has been temporarily suspended due to a suspicious frogging incident.

ABOUT THE PUBLISHER

C ity Owl Press is a cutting edge indie publishing company, bringing the world of romance and speculative fiction to discerning readers.

www.cityowlpress.com

CPSIA information can be obtained
at www.ICGtesting.com
Printed in the USA
LVOW03s1428270717
542420LV00001B/4/P